365

Adventure Stories

OmKIDZ | **Om Books International**

Reprinted in 2020

Corporate & Editorial Office
A-12, Sector 64, Noida 201 301
Uttar Pradesh, India
Phone: +91 120 477 4100
Email: editorial@ombooks.com
Website: www.ombooksinternational.com

Sales Office
107, Ansari Road, Darya Ganj
New Delhi 110 002, India
Phone: +91 11 4000 9000
Email: sales@ombooks.com

© Om Books International 2014

ISBN: 978-93-84225-32-2

Printed in China

10 9 8 7 6 5 4

365
Adventure Stories

Om
KIDZ
An imprint of Om Books International

Contents

December

1. Naughty Bobo

Bobo the puppy was a very naughty little dog. He kept getting into mischief. One afternoon, Bobo's owner brought him inside the house. "Bobo, you must stay at home today," he said. "It's going to rain." Bobo wagged his tail and sat in his spot obediently, but he was already thinking of a plan to sneak out. Finally, Bobo got his chance. He quickly slipped out when his owner opened the door for the postman. Bobo started splashing about in the rain happily. In no time, he was covered in mud. After jumping and playing, he was very tired. But when he tried to go home, Bobo realised that he was lost. He got scared and started whining. Just then, a little girl spotted him and picked him up. She put him in her basket and began walking away. Bobo did not know where she would take him, but he went along because he was scared of being alone in the dark. Tired, he fell asleep in the basket. When he woke up, he found himself in his own house. The girl was his owner's cousin who had come to stay. She had arrived after Bobo ran away. Bobo was happy to return home and promised never to be naughty again.

1

2. The Scary Mask

Annie and Minnie were afraid of the dark. The reflections from the window would make shadows on their bedroom wall. The sisters thought that they were monsters.

One day, Annie had an idea. "Let's make a scary-looking mask," she said. "That will shoo away the monsters!" Her sister agreed enthusiastically. Annie and Minnie set to work. They drew the mask on a large sheet of paper and decorated it with chocolate wrappers and glitter. When it was complete, they hung it up.

That night, the two sisters were eager to check if the mask worked. They jumped into bed and switched off the light. "It's working!" said Minnie, clapping her hands. The mask was blocking the reflections from the window.

The sisters slept soundly ever since.

3. Adamo's Favourite Painting

Adamo was a poor but talented artist. One day, he painted a beautiful painting.

"This is my best work!" he said and hung it proudly over his bed. Sadly, Adamo could not pay his house rent. He had to leave the house and his painting behind. But he did not lose hope and started working even harder. Soon, he became rich and famous. Even then, he never forgot his favourite painting. Adamo searched all the art galleries for it, but he had no luck.

One day, Adamo was browsing an antique shop. He saw a familiar painting under a big pile of rubbish. It was his favourite painting!

"How strange," he thought. "Everyone wants to buy my paintings, but nobody cares for my best work."

4. Becky and the Talking Hat

Becky loved all kinds of clothes. One day, she found an old, dusty hat in the attic. As soon as she put it on, a voice boomed out from the hat. "Hey, be gentle," it said. "I'm old!"

Becky gasped. A talking hat!

The hat continued speaking. "Let me tell you about my adventure," it said. "It is about my first owner. I was happy when he bought me. But soon, I realised that he was on his way to rob a shop.

He only bought me to hide his face.

I decided to stop him. When he robbed the shop and started running, I jumped off his head. Everyone saw his face. The police caught him easily!"

5. Grandma's Cat Statue

Grandma gave Bobby a cat statue for Christmas. This made him upset. "I wanted a toy jeep," he said. "Or something adventurous like that!" Grandma only smiled. "This cat is also adventurous," she said. "Let me tell you its story."

The cat statue was created in Ancient Egypt, where they worshipped cats like Gods.

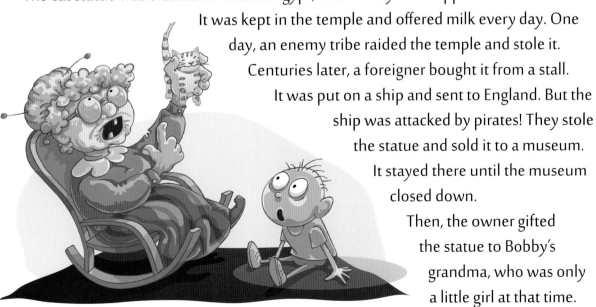

It was kept in the temple and offered milk every day. One day, an enemy tribe raided the temple and stole it.

Centuries later, a foreigner bought it from a stall.

It was put on a ship and sent to England. But the ship was attacked by pirates! They stole the statue and sold it to a museum.

It stayed there until the museum closed down.

Then, the owner gifted the statue to Bobby's grandma, who was only a little girl at that time.

6. The Postcard

James went to the shop and bought a yellow postcard. He was going to send it to his friend John on his birthday. The postcard had a nice birthday message on one side and John's address on the other.

The yellow postcard couldn't wait to reach John. It wanted to see John's face as he got his birthday message. The yellow postcard went from the mailbox to the mail truck and was finally put into the postman's mail bag.

It was the day of John's birthday and the postcard was happy that it had reached on time. That afternoon, when they reached John's front door, the postman did something odd. He put the postcard back in the mail bag. The yellow postcard was furious. What a mean postman!

But then, the postman went to the next house and knocked on the door. "Birthday mail for John!" he said. "Your friend got the wrong house number."

The yellow postcard realised it was being given to John. It was thrilled to see John's shining eyes on seeing it. John was happy and so was the postcard.

7. What's for Breakfast?

Mia's mother had gone away for the weekend. That left Mia alone at home with her father. Mia's mother used to make her breakfast every morning. But that Saturday, she ran into the kitchen to find that the table had no food on it. Only her father was sitting there, reading the newspaper. "Good morning, dad," she said. "What's for breakfast?" Sadly, Mia's dad was a disaster in the kitchen. He said, "How about I take you out for breakfast?" But Mia was too hungry. She did not want to wait. "Let's cook something together instead," she replied. They started looking for ingredients. Mia took out eggs, bread, tomatoes and cheese. Her dad found some onions and butter. "Now what do we do with these?" he wondered aloud.

They tried roasting, boiling and baking their ingredients, but they ended up burning everything. Finally, they decided to make a big omelette with cheese, bits of onions and tomatoes. They toasted the bread to go with it. The omelette was delicious and Mia was happy that she and her father finally got their breakfast right.

8. Whodunit?

When Joel came home from school one day, he found that his mother was annoyed. "Who made that mess?" she asked, pointing to her tangled knitting wool.

"I don't know," replied Joel. Mother was very puzzled. She untangled the wool and kept it neatly. But the next day, she saw that it was tangled again! "I have to get to the bottom of this," she thought.

On the third day, Joel's mother stayed in the kitchen all morning, quietly keeping watch. After a while, she saw the neighbour's kitten scramble in through the window. She settled on top of the wool, batting and chewing at it until she was tired. Then she went back out.

Mother couldn't wait to tell Joel how she found the culprit!

6

9. Camping Out

During the holidays, Kate would love to sleep outside the house in her tent. It made her feel like she was camping in the woods. One night, she woke up feeling thirsty.

But she remembered that she had forgotten her water bottle in the fridge.

Kate crept into the house, tiptoeing to the kitchen. Just as she was picking up the bottle, she felt something soft hit her. She thought she was imagining it. But it hit her again!

She screamed and started hitting back.

The kitchen then filled with light. Kate's parents had heard the noise and had come down. That's when they saw Kate's little brother hitting her with his pillow. He had heard the noises and thought she was a burglar!

10. The Night in the Library

When Tina went to school one morning, she thought it would be an ordinary day. But when it was time for recess, the teacher said, "Kids, don't play outside today. It's raining very heavily!" The kids sat in class all day. Tina hoped that it would stop raining soon, so that she could play outside for a little while.

But the rain didn't stop. Soon, it was completely flooded. The water was almost up to the children's knees! All of them had to stay in school that night. They spent their evening doing their homework and playing indoor games.

Soon, it was time to sleep. Tina was thrilled when she was given a place in the library. Before lights went out, Tina decided to do some night-time reading. She went to her favourite aisle that had books. She picked a book and started reading. Before she knew it, she had fallen fast asleep!

Her teacher found her there the next morning, curled up with the book.

Tina was not scared of sleeping alone in a library aisle. In fact, she quite enjoyed her night in the library.

7

11. In the Jungle

Aaron was very excited. His uncle worked as a forest ranger. He was going to take him and his friends on a jungle safari.

On the day of the safari, they all piled into Aaron's uncle's jeep and rode around the jungle. They saw all kinds of animals like monkeys, elephants and giraffes.

Most of the animals stayed far away, but the monkeys came very close to their jeep. They were naughty and not afraid of people. When they stopped to take pictures, a monkey swooped down and grabbed Aaron's camera. He flung it into the bushes and scampered off. Aaron was very upset.

His camera was precious to him.

"Cheer up, Aaron," said his uncle. "Maybe we can find it." Aaron's uncle made them wait outside while he went into the thick shrubs. Suddenly, he called out to them. "Come here!" he called. "I've found an old temple!"

The temple was crumbling and forgotten, but they could still see the beautiful designs and carvings.

"Kids, we may not find the camera, but we have found an ancient marvel!" said Aaron's uncle.

8

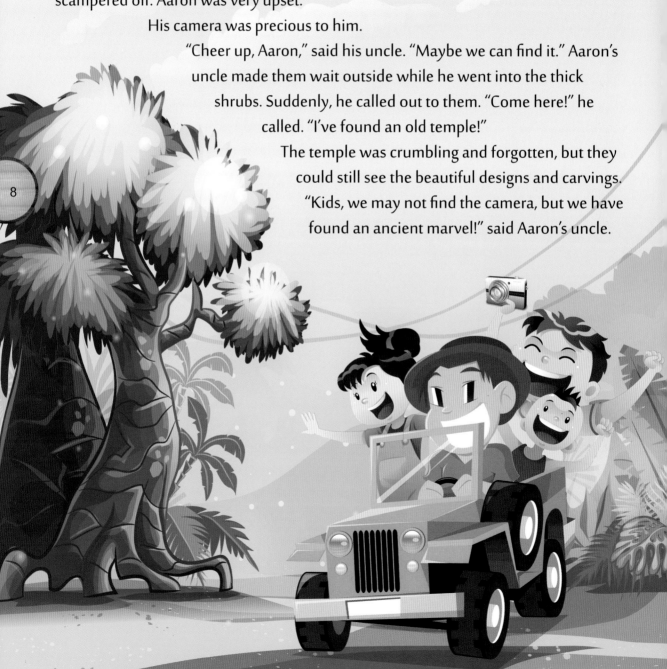

12. Butterfingers

One afternoon, Billy came home to find his mother frantically searching for something. "What are you looking for, Mom?" he asked.

"I'm looking for a receipt," she replied. "Can you help me search for it?"

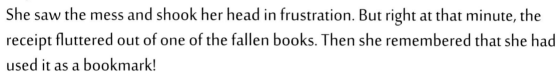

Billy looked over the fridge, under the sofa and on the kitchen shelves. Then, he started looking on the bookshelves. As he tried to look under a stack of books, Billy ended up toppling the entire pile. THUD! They all fell down.

Billy's mother heard the commotion and ran inside. She saw the mess and shook her head in frustration. But right at that minute, the receipt fluttered out of one of the fallen books. Then she remembered that she had used it as a bookmark!

If it hadn't been for Billy's clumsiness, she would not have found her receipt!

13. Jake in a New City

Jake was visiting his cousins and uncle. To reach their house, he had to take a train. He was nervous because he had never travelled by train before.

Jake boarded the train and decided to ask the boy in front of him for help.

"I'm getting off at the same stop," said the boy. "I'll help you out."

When Jake told the boy his uncle's address, the boy gasped. "This is my address!" he cried. "Are you my cousin Jake?"

Jake had not met his cousin since they were very little and they had both failed to recognise each other!

Marvelling at the happy coincidence, they went home together.

14. Overcoming Fear

For his New Year's resolution, Jim decided that he would overcome his fear of spiders. So, Jim's father drove him to a university nearby to meet a professor of arachnology, which is the study of spiders. The professor's office was filled with glass cases, each housing a different kind of spider. When Jim saw them, he got goosebumps and his face lost all its colour. After some coaxing, Jim agreed to hold a spider. When his father placed the spider on his palm, Jim saw that there was nothing to be scared of. The spider would not hurt him. It just walked around on Jim's palm, tickling him with its big, furry legs.

When he had finished playing, Jim put the spider back in its case. That is how he got over his fear of spiders!

15. The Magic Goblet

One night, Gordo the goblin was walking through a forest, looking for magical flowers. Suddenly, he saw a little blue bird that was tangled in a clump of vines. Gordo stopped and set the bird free. "Thank you!" chirped the bird. "As a reward, I will enchant any object that you wish."

Gordo only had his basket of magical flowers and his favourite goblet. He allowed the bird to enchant the goblet.

He took the enchanted goblet home and found out that it immediately filled up with whichever drink he asked for. Gordo and his family never went thirsty again!

16. How to Become a Dragon

The dragon is the most legendary and majestic creature in the animal kingdom. But here is the greatest secret—no animal is born a dragon. An animal must become a dragon.

To become a dragon, animals must have attained two years of age. They also should have been good children and good students. Once they have met these requirements, the animals must travel to the big, wide forest and journey to the Yellow River. During the journey—which may take a year or two—the animals must have made at least five good friends, helped at least seven animals and learnt at least three new skills. Only once the animals meet these conditions will a secret path to the Yellow River waterfall reveal itself. At the waterfall, the animals must swim or climb against the strong current. This is the most difficult part, as the waterfall is very treacherous. Only the animals who reach the top and answer the questions of the Voice from Heaven become dragons.

It sounds easy, doesn't it? But keep in mind that we have not had a dragon for more than a hundred centuries!

17. The Dream Adventures

Abby stayed home from school because she was very ill. She was upset because her class was going on a field trip to the museum. Abby really wanted to see the Egyptian temple exhibit! She snuggled in bed and cried herself to sleep.

When she woke up, she found that she was standing outside an Egyptian temple. Abby was very confused. Then, she spotted her friend, Tim, walking towards her. "Hello Abby!" he said. "Did you miss the field trip, too?"

"Yes, I am ill," replied Abby. "But where are we?"

"We are in Dreamland!" said Tim. "When children fall sick and go to sleep, they visit different places in Dreamland."

Abby was excited. "I can't wait to start exploring!" she said. But when she tried to enter the temple, she was stopped by a creature with a man's head and a lion's body. "I am a sphinx," it said. "I will only allow you inside if you answer my riddle! Tommy's mother has three children. The first child is called April. The second is called May. What is the third child called?"

Abby thought hard until she got the answer. "Tommy!" she said. She was right! The sphinx let them in. Abby explored the temple all day and fell asleep inside it.

When she woke up, she was back in her room and feeling much better.

18. Abby Aboard the Pirate Ship

The next day, Abby eagerly settled in bed and fell asleep soon. When she woke up, she found that the floor beneath her was gently rocking. Tim was sleeping nearby. Abby shook him awake. "Wake up," she said. "I think we're on a ship!"

Tim shot up immediately. Just then, they heard footsteps behind them. When they turned around, they saw an angry-looking pirate standing before them. Abby and Tim were shocked. But the pirate burst into jolly laughter. "I scared the stuffing out of you!" he said. "My name's Captain Sunny. We need your help!"

The kids followed him to the deck and saw more mean-looking pirates around. But when they spoke to them, they saw that the pirates were all kind and harmless. "The pirate Brutus has stolen our treasure map," said Captain Sunny. "He will only return it if we send him the answer to this maths problem. Will you help us?"

The problem was simple. The pirates could not solve it because they had not gone to school. Abby and Tim solved the problem with ease.

They sent the solution to Brutus with the parrot and waited with bated breath for his reply. Finally, they saw the little green bird flying back with the map tied to its leg. Everyone cheered for Abby and Tim!

13

19. Abby and the Special Flower

Abby woke up in a forest the next day. Tim was not there because he was already feeling well. Abby wandered around alone, until she saw a handsome prince on a horse. "I'm Prince Ridesalot," he said. "I think you've been sent here to help me."

"It would be my pleasure," said Abby. "Tell me your problem."

The prince explained that he was in love with a beautiful princess and wanted to woo her. "I've tried giving her flowers," he said. "But she rejects them all."

"Hmm," said Abby. "Tell me a little about this princess." The prince said that her name was Princess Readsalottie and she loved chemistry experiments. Abby had an idea. "Why not give her a flower that she can perform experiments on?" she asked.

"The sakura would be perfect. She could extract the flavour and use it for cooking or even as perfume!"

So Prince Ridesalot went all the way to Japan and came back with the flowers. As you can imagine, the princess loved the flower! She loved it so much that she renamed the kingdom Sakura.

14

20. Abby and the Dancing Spider

The next day, Abby knew that it was her last day in Dreamland, as she was getting better very quickly. She woke up in a village of dancing people. Everyone looked very tired from dancing, but they seemed very happy to see her.

"Hello there!" he said. "There's an evil, monstrous spider who is tormenting us. It makes us dance outside its cave all night for its amusement. We are so tired! Please help us."

Abby decided to teach the spider a lesson. The spider worried the villagers at night and slept all day. As it lay snoring, Abby crept inside its cave and put rollerblades on each of its eight legs. When the spider woke up and tried to walk, it kept sliding and slipping! It could not stay still. It was forced to keep moving all night.

By sunrise, it was so tired that it begged the villagers to untie the rollerblades. Then, Abby went to him. "Now that you know how it feels," said Abby, "Promise us that you will not force the villagers to dance all night. Only then will I untie the rollerblades."

The spider promised to be good to the villagers and Abby took the skates off. That was the last time the spider troubled the villagers!

21. The Thief of Littleville

There was a thief in the village of Littleville and the villagers did not know how to stop him. Each morning, one household or another would find some food missing. This had been going on for a week.

Finally, the elders came up with a plan. They told every household to paint a layer of red paint around their food. The thief would get paint on his feet and be easily caught.

The next morning, all the kids were found with red feet! The children explained that they had found a wounded lion near the edge of the forest and were afraid the elders would kill it. So, they would steal food for the animal. The elders applauded the children for their kind spirit.

22. The Blue Pill

Fred was a naughty child. His grandparents told him not to play with their pills, but he would not listen. He was fascinated with the different shapes and colours. He thought that they were used to make food tasty.

One day, Fred stole a blue pill from his grandpa's pill box and mixed it in his orange juice. He gulped down the juice and ran off to play. Almost immediately, Fred's stomach started rumbling. He ran to the toilet. But it happened over and over again!

Poor Fred was in a fix. He went to his grandpa and explained what he had done. Fred's grandpa just chuckled. He explained that the blue pill was a medicine that made you want to go to the toilet. So Fred had to spend the whole day running to the toilet and back.

23. The Balloon

A big red balloon had been blown up an hour ago, inside a house. But it was already restless. It wanted to go out and see the big, wide world! After a while, a gentle breeze wafted through the room. The balloon saw his chance to escape. It quickly sat on the breeze and floated out of the window. All morning, the balloon floated over a big park, a flyover and a parking lot. It was fascinated, but it wanted to see more. However, it got stuck between the branches of a tree, next to a crow. The crow took the balloon's string in its beak and flew away. They flew over a train track, a playground and even saw the airport.

The crow grew tired and yawned, opening his beak wide. The balloon was free again! It wandered away idly, taking in the beautiful sights. Suddenly, it saw the most beautiful sight—golden sand and blue water stretching as far as it could see. It was the beach! The balloon went straight towards the sparkling sea and bobbed on the waves. It was finally happy.

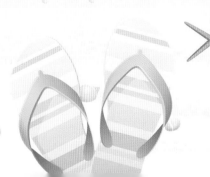

24. The Brave Brothers

Two brothers, Ben and Owen, were staying at a beautiful resort during their vacation. One day, they heard a lady shouting outside. They ran out to see that her puppy was stranded on a rock in the pond. The pond was deep and not meant for swimming. The brothers decided that they would rescue the puppy. Ben tied a rope around

Owen's waist with a strong knot. He then tied the rope to a thick branch of a nearby tree. Owen was a swimming champion in school. He swam to the rock and brought the puppy back.

The little puppy licked both their faces and wagged its little tail. The lady treated the boys to big ice cream sundaes.

25. Trapping a Tiger

Jack's village was being pestered by a tiger from the forest nearby. The tiger would come in every night and steal a sheep or a goat. The villagers were afraid that the tiger would, one day, take one of the children!

They called for a meeting for ideas. Jack raised his hand. "I have a plan," he said. "We need to buy a few kilos of meat from the butcher. Then, we will inject the meat with a strong tranquiliser. We will place this meat near the forest entrance and let the tiger eat it up. When he falls asleep, we will capture him. Then we can call the wildlife preservation authorities to come here and take him to the reserve."

The villagers applauded Jack's smart plan. With his help, they caught the tiger and sent it to a sanctuary. Jack became the village hero.

26. The Tooth Fairy's Problem

The village of Sweetville had lots of children with wobbly teeth. The Tooth Fairy was very happy with this. She was doing great business! She would collect at least five teeth every night. What's more, the kids loved her because she always left a coin and a pamphlet about oral hygiene under their pillows.

But then, a new dentist came to the village. All the kids adored him more. He lovingly removed their wobbly teeth while making them laugh at his silly faces. When he was done, he would then give them an ice cream and a pamphlet about oral hygiene.

The Tooth Fairy's tooth collection had reduced. She didn't know what to do! She decided to confront the dentist and make him leave the village. But the minute they saw each other, the Tooth Fairy and the dentist fell in love.

Soon, they were married. For each tooth, they would give the kids a coin, an ice cream and a pamphlet. The dentist would then give all the teeth to his wife. They were a perfect couple and they lived happily ever after.

19

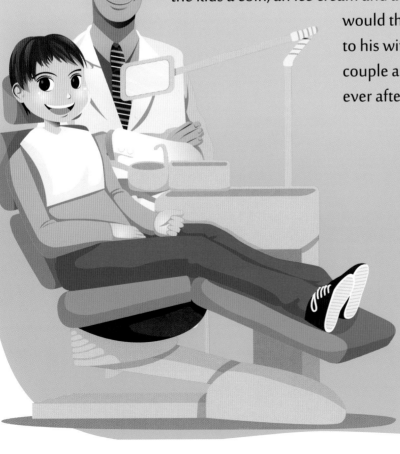

27. The Toy Engine's Birthday

It was the night before Eugene the toy engine's birthday. He was very excited to receive wishes and gifts from the other toys.

At midnight, all the toys went up to Eugene. "Can you give us a ride to the doll house?" they asked. "We have a meeting there tonight." Eugene the engine was shocked. He thought they had come to wish him!

"Have a seat," he told the toys, grinding his teeth. When they sat down, Eugene sped off. Instead of taking them to the doll house, he went in the opposite direction. All the toys started panicking. "Stop, Eugene," they shouted. "You're going the wrong way!" But Eugene paid no attention to them.

Once Eugene had let out all his steam, he turned to his friends. "I was upset because you have forgotten my birthday," he said. The toys looked at each other with guilty expressions. "You're right, Eugene," they replied. "Why don't we discuss a suitable punishment for us at the meeting?"

20

Eugene agreed and finally took the toys to the right destination. As soon as they reached the doll house, the toys switched the lights on and yelled, "Surprise!" They had thrown him a surprise party!

Eugene was so thrilled. He apologised for his behaviour and enjoyed his party.

28. Wally and the Snake

Wally was a city boy. He had hardly seen any wildlife, except in the zoo and on television. His parents took him to a wildlife resort for his summer vacation so that he could experience the wonders of nature.

One afternoon, Wally went for a walk without informing his parents. A few minutes down a trail, he spotted a huge snake. Poor Wally didn't know what to do. He stood transfixed on the spot.

The snake raised its head and angrily stared at Wally. It was just about to strike when a man sneaked up to it from behind and expertly caught it.

The man was one of the authorities at the resort. He took the snake away immediately. Wally was relieved. He learnt not to go wandering by himself.

29. The Caffeine Kick

Teresa wanted to try her father's black coffee, but he never allowed her. One day, Teresa's father left for work in a hurry and left his coffee unfinished. She saw her chance and drank the whole thing in one gulp. It was bitter and tasted horrid.

Later, Teresa began to sweat. Then her fingers began to quiver. She ran to her mother. "Mummy," she cried. "I drank daddy's coffee. Now I feel like jumping and vomiting at the same time!"

"Don't worry," said her mother. "The bad feeling will go away." Teresa bounced on her bed. Then, she ran up and down the stairs till her feet ached.

Finally, she threw up. Her mother helped her clean up and tucked her in bed. She wouldn't drink daddy's coffee again!

30. A Picnic for One

Jenny was sad. All her friends had gone away for holidays, leaving her alone. She had nobody to play with. "Why don't you have a picnic on your own?" suggested her mother. "You can go to the lake and enjoy yourself." Jenny packed a few books and a basket full of delicious food, and set out.

As soon as she sat down, Jenny saw an egret swoop down and pluck a fish out of the lake. Next, a rabbit hopped out of its burrow and peeked inside her basket. But when Jenny leaned closer, the rabbit scurried away like its tail was on fire!

She lay on her back and saw a mighty eagle perched on a branch above her. It had a wriggling snake in its beak. The eagle almost dropped it and Jenny thought it would land on her head! But the eagle caught it at the last moment.

Jenny was fascinated with everything she had seen. Before she knew it, the Sun had begun to set and she had to go home. She told her mother all about her picnic and never complained about being alone!

22

31. The No-light Night

One evening, Reggie's parents went out for a wedding. He was home alone, watching a football match on television. Suddenly, the lights went out. Looking outside, it was clear that the electricity along the whole street had gone out.

Reggie was very scared of the dark. He crept into his bed and prayed that his parents would return soon. As he sat there shaking like a leaf, he heard a knock on the door. Reggie was petrified. He knew it could not be his parents, as they had the keys. After a while, the knocking stopped. Reggie sighed with relief and continued waiting. Just as he heard his parents opening the door, the electricity returned. Reggie ran to hug his parents and told them all about the strange knocking. That's when it happened again!

This time, Reggie's father opened the door. To Reggie's surprise, his father let out a roar of laughter. It had been the old lady next door who had knocked. She was worried about Reggie and had come to check on him. If only Reggie had been a little brave, he would have had company on that pitch black night.

23

1. The Bumbling Magician

There was once a magician who wasn't doing very well. His shows were no longer popular with the people. "Don't worry, sir," said Mr. Tibbs, his faithful assistant. "Just believe in the power of magic!"

Mr. Tibbs loved magic and he wanted to be a magician one day. However, he was terribly clumsy and absent-minded. He would keep mixing all the spells and tricks. One day, the magician refused to perform. Only 10 people had come to watch his show. He handed his wand to Mr. Tibbs, saying, "You perform. I'm too upset."

Mr. Tibbs took the stage, nervous but excited. For his first trick, he was going to pull a rabbit out of his hat. But poor Mr. Tibbs pulled out a rat instead! He was so surprised that he shrieked and jumped as the rat scurried off the stage.

The audience laughed harder than they ever had before! They loved Mr. Tibbs' antics and told all their friends about his show, which had both magic and comedy.

2. The Thoughtful Gift

Mother's Day was coming up and Tammy was all out of ideas. The previous year, she cooked her mother breakfast. Before that, she'd painted her a beautiful picture. And before that, she'd grown her a flowering plant. Finally, Tammy decided to make her mother a booklet of coupons. On each coupon, she wrote a different message. One said, "One relaxing foot massage." Another said, "One personal assistant for a day."

Tammy's mother was thrilled to receive such a thoughtful gift. "Thank you, dear," she said to Tammy, giving her a hug. "I'm sure we'll have a good time using these coupons together!"

3. The Kidnapping

Pearl belonged to a very rich family. One day, as she got into the car after school, she was surprised to see a new face behind the wheel. "Your regular driver is unwell," said the stranger. "I am his replacement for today."

Pearl was suspicious. When the man was not looking, she quickly sent a message to her father, explaining the situation.

As they left the school, the man's friendly behaviour disappeared. He snatched her phone away and began driving away. But Pearl's father had already alerted the police. In no time, they caught up with the car and arrested the man.

They congratulated Pearl on being smart and alert.

4. The Naughty Keyboard

Bezzil the wizard lived in an enchanted house. Every item in his house had a mind of its own. Bezzil just had to ask the kitchen to cook him some food and everything would come together to fix him a delicious meal. He would ask his television for something to cheer him up and it would switch to his favourite comedy show. However, Bezzil's computer keyboard was a naughty one. It would mess around with Bezzil's mails and create a lot of trouble.

One day, Bezzil typed a mail to the packers and movers. He wanted to transport a table to his brother in Antarctica. The keyboard was bored and decided to be naughty. Without reading the mail, it replaced the table's name with its own.

A while later, the movers came and started packing the keyboard. The keyboard yelped and cried. "I don't want to go to Antarctica!" it said. "There's been a mistake!" But the movers paid no heed. "Bezzil's mail said to ship you off to Antarctica," they said.

Just then, Bezzil entered and saw what was happening. He set things right and had the table shipped off. The keyboard learnt its lesson and tried to be a little less naughty.

26

5. Grandma's Cellphone

Grandma was always misplacing her cellphone. She would keep asking her grandchildren, Maria and Charlie, to look for it. And they would find it in the strangest of places. Once, they even found it in the fridge!

One day, Grandma lost her phone again. Maria and Charlie immediately started to look for it. When the children called Grandma's phone, they could not hear it anywhere in the house. They looked in the fridge, in the microwave, in the washing machine, in the laundry basket and on every kitchen shelf. But they had no luck. Grandma was upset. She sat down with Maria and Charlie, and together, they thought about where it could be. Just then, their pet dog scampered inside, covered in mud. The two children exchanged a knowing glance. They were both thinking the same thing! They ran outside at once.

Sure enough, they saw the phone sticking out of the mud near the rose bush. They took the phone back to Grandma, who laughed when she heard that her phone had been buried like a bone. For once, the dog was to blame and not Grandma!

27

6. Sacrifice

"O great Gods of the Sun and the Moon, here is our sacrifice to you. We will burn this little boy, so that you bless us with joy!" the savages chanted, ignoring Jay's shouts. He was tied to a pole and all the savages were dancing energetically around him. Their faces were painted with lines and they had feathers stuck in their hair. They carried spears and glowered ferociously as they circled Jay.

Poor Jay was struggling against the ropes. "Don't kill me!" he cried. "Somebody save me!" But the savages just laughed. "Nobody can hear you, little boy!" they said. "It is time for you to burn, so that the Gods can eat you up!"

Just then, a voice was heard from the distance. "Enough of your game!" it said. "Untie your brother and come for lunch!"

All the savages—and Jay—groaned loudly. They were having such a good time! "Last one in is a rotten egg!" yelled one of the kids, as they raced into the house.

7. Loch Ness

Max and Julia were visiting their friends, Olivia and Rhys, in the Scottish Highlands. One day, they went to the famous Loch Ness, which is a huge lake. According to a legend, a huge dinosaur-like creature called the Loch Ness monster lived there. The kids had decided to capture the monster, but they could not decide how to do it.

"Let's coax it out with food," said Julia.

"No!" said Rhys. "Let's drain the lake!"

"Wait a minute," said Max. "Even if we do capture the monster, what are we going to do with it?" All the kids scratched their heads. They could not think of anything! In the end, they decided to just leave the monster where it was.

8. Hiding Treasure

Adam's cousin, George, was coming to stay with him for a few days. He did not want George touching his priced toys and breaking them. So, he put his favourite toys into his old lunchbox and looked for a place to hide it.

Adam could not bury it in the garden because his dog would dig it up.

He could not hide it under his bed because George would surely look there.

Then, an idea stuck Adam. Once George arrived and unpacked his bag, Adam hid his box into George's empty bag!

George kept looking for Adam's toys, but he had no luck. He never once considered looking into his own bag!

9. The Singing Frogs

The forest frogs formed a musical band and they were very good. Their tunes were groovy and they played at every party in the forest. But the band had big dreams. They wanted to become famous outside the forest, too.

So the frogs sat on the river bank and performed for all the boats that passed by. Finally, they got their break. A movie producer heard the frogs and was very impressed.

He took the frogs to Hollywood. If you have ever watched a movie about a little mermaid, you may have seen the frogs performing. They finally got their moment in the limelight!

10. The Other Senses

After her eye operation, the doctor had bandaged Gemma's eyes. She sat on the hospital bed, feeling miserable. She wanted to watch television!

"Gemma!" her doctor called. "Who am I?"

"You're my doctor," replied Gemma.

"Right," he said. "What flower is this?" Gemma sniffed the vase. "It's a rose!" she said. Then, the doctor placed something in Gemma's hand.

"What did I give you?" he asked.

"A grape!" said Gemma, popping it in her mouth.

"See?" said the doctor. "You can use your other senses to have fun!" Gemma spent the whole day hearing, sniffing, feeling and tasting different things. It was a fantastic day!

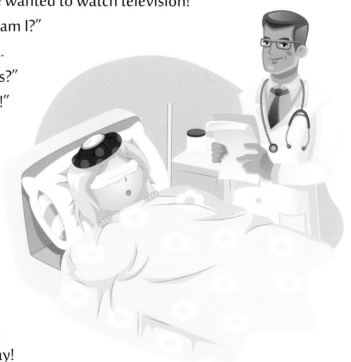

11. Hello Halloween

Bubble the bear cub loved eating candy. But he could never find enough candy in the forest. Bubble had to make do with the stuff that kids left behind when they came camping. But it wasn't enough! Bubble wanted more candy and so he hatched a plan. Bubble decided that he would have to sneak into town where people lived. They had lots of candy there. But he had to be careful. If the people saw him, he would be taken away and put in a zoo. Bubble decided to go at night, when people would not be able to see him clearly. And what better night than Halloween night!

People would not even know that Bubble was a bear. They would think that he was a little child in a very scary and realistic bear costume.

On Halloween, Bubble took a bucket and went trick-or-treating from door to door. Nobody paid him much attention. They just dumped candy into his bucket and wished him Happy Halloween. Some even complimented him for his costume!

Bubble's bucket was overflowing. He had enough candy to keep him happy for the whole year.

31

12. The Dragon Recipe

"AAH!" screamed the little girl, pointing to the wall. "It's a chameleon!" Ronny the chameleon crept away sadly. Nobody liked him. He didn't want to be a chameleon anymore. He wanted to be a dragon. Everyone liked dragons! "But how do I become a dragon?" Ronny wondered. After thinking hard, Ronny decided that he had to learn two things—how to breathe out fire and how to fly. Ronny decided that first he would learn how to breathe out fire. But no matter how much he tried, he could not produce anything more than a burp.

Finally, he got an idea. Ronny had overheard his mother complain about his father's cooking once. She had said, "This food is so spicy, I'll soon breathe fire!" So Ronny went to the kitchen to create a fire-breathing potion. He mashed hot peppers, chilli powder, ginger powder and fresh chillies together in a bowl. To that, he added hot water. When Ronny tasted it, his face went bright red! His eyes began to water. He started running around and yelling his head off. Ronny's grandmother came running inside. She made him drink a glass of cold milk. That's how Ronny realised that it wasn't so easy to become a dragon!

13. Bathing Bruno

Bruno was a playful dog. He liked to go scampering about and playing in the dirt. But he didn't like taking baths. Even the word would send him running away!

One day, Bruno saw his mistress coming towards him to give him a bath. So he ran up the stairs. When she came after him, he ran into the closet. From there, he ran to the kitchen and hid behind the dustbin. Bruno chuckled to himself, thinking that nobody would find him. But then, he saw his master and mistress come from either side! They picked him up and carried him to the bathroom. Poor Bruno knew he was defeated. But at least he was clean!

14. Baby Dragon

Josh and Jenna explored the wooded areas around their house, when Jenna stumbled and fell down. "What is this big rock doing in my way?" she said.

But when they had a closer look, they saw that it was a huge egg! It was so big that Jenna and Josh had to carry it home together. They kept it by the fireplace to keep it warm.

Soon, the egg hatched. And to their great surprise, a baby dragon popped out! At first, Jenna and Josh were scared of it. But the baby dragon was harmless. It wouldn't breathe fire on them or hurt them.

In no time, Jenna and Josh had become good friends with the baby dragon. The dragon took them for long rides and helped them heat their food! They had a lot of fun together.

15. The Vampire's Dilemma

Little Franck hated the taste of blood, even though he was a vampire. He preferred drinking grape juice. During meals, he would only pretend to drink blood. He would actually just feed all the blood to his pet bat under the table. He had a stash of juice boxes in his bedroom so he wouldn't go hungry.

One day, Franck ran out of grape juice. He went to the store and brought a new carton to hide in his bedroom. He returned home to find his mother standing at the door. He hid the carton in a bush so that she wouldn't see it.

"What's that you were carrying?" asked his mother when he reached.

"Nothing, Mom," lied Franck.

Later that night, when Franck crept back outside to get his carton, he found that it was not there! He returned home sadly.

To his surprise, he found the whole family sitting at the table with his missing carton on it.

Franck hung his head and prepared himself for a scolding.

"You know," said his father. "If you didn't like blood, you could've just told us. I've been drinking beetroot juice for years!"

16. The Ambitious Ant

Anton the ant was an ambitious fellow. He wanted to be the first ant on the Moon. All the television channels were going on and on about the rocket that was scheduled to go to the Moon next week. Anton decided to go with it. So, he packed his bags and travelled to the launch base. When the rocket was about to be launched, he climbed on and latched onto it. After the countdown, the rocket shot off. But Anton saw that part by part, portions of the rocket detached themselves and fell back to Earth. Before he could scamper any higher, the part he was on also detached itself and fell down.

Luckily, Anton fell next to his house and was safe. Even though he did not reach the Moon, he was certainly the only ant to have gone that high.

35

17. The Vengeful Vines

Goggy the gnome didn't pay much attention as he walked to work and back. On his way, there was a curved bend where a vine was trying to creep towards a big tree. Goggy would step on the vine every day as he passed by.

One day, when he was returning home, he felt his foot getting stuck. He was unable to lift it up. Before he could set his left foot free, his right foot also got ensnared. The vine crept around his feet and held him hostage.

Goggy tried to yank his feet out, but the vine held him tightly. Finally, after much begging and pleading, the vine set him free. From then on, Goggy paid more attention when he walked!

18. Trading Pets

Paul the giant and Peter the elf were best friends. They decided to exchange pets for a day. Paul had to take home Peter's little bird and Peter's guest was Paul's elephant. It was very chaotic! Paul kept losing sight of the bird. He had to be careful not to step on it! Peter was having a tough time, too. He couldn't even fit the elephant through his door. He had to be kept in the garden. Whatever food Peter gave him, the elephant would swallow it in a second and ask for more.

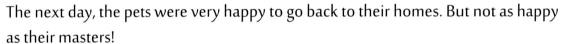

The next day, the pets were very happy to go back to their homes. But not as happy as their masters!

36

19. The Angry Venus Flytrap

The Venus flytrap at the edge of the woods was known for its bad temper. When it got angry, it would snap at anything that was nearby. Once, it even tried to eat Mr. Rabbit! On one hot day, the Venus flytrap was especially angry.

It wanted ice cream but the ice cream truck had not come yet. When it finally showed up, the Venus flytrap started yelling and chomping away at anything it could reach.

It took a few seconds for it to realise that it was chomping its own second head off! It burst out laughing and has been more cool-tempered since then.

20. Enchanted Running Shoes

Daedalus went to Pockharts School of Magic. The school had organised a race in which the students had to enchant an object to help them win. Daedalus had spent many weeks enchanting his running shoes until they could make him run very fast. But there was one problem—the shoes had a habit of running away on their own. And that's exactly what they did on the morning of the race! Daedalus hunted for them high and low, but in vain. As he stood at the starting line, he felt very silly. His friends all had their enchanted objects—one had a magic broom, another had a super-fast skateboard and one kid even had a pair of enchanted wings.

As the whistle was blown, all the kids took off. Daedalus had no choice but to run on his two feet. All the kids raced ahead of him. Just then, out of the blue, his shoes came running towards him! Daedalus put them on quickly. The second he tied his laces, he ran faster than all the other kids. His naughty shoes did help him win after all!

21. Komodo Dragons

Uncle Tony was a wildlife photographer. He always told Penny interesting stories. One day, he was telling her about his adventures in Indonesia.

"I went to the island of Komodo," he said. "I wanted to photograph the largest lizard in the world—the Komodo dragon!"

"Woah!" said Penny. "A fire-breathing dragon?"

Uncle Tony laughed. "Not really," he said. "It's a huge lizard with a deadly bite."

He then continued his story. "As I was looking around," he said, "I heard my partner call out. I turned and saw that there was a Komodo dragon right behind me, eyeing me like a tasty treat! I didn't know what to do! I had no weapons, but I had some extra-strong mints in my pocket, so I flung those at it. The lizard licked the mint. It shuddered at the taste and slunk away. I was safe! And I learnt that if you invite a Komodo dragon for dinner, you shouldn't serve it anything minty!"

38

22. Grapes and Raisins

On a hot summer afternoon, Gary's mother gave him a plate of grapes to eat. He ate most of the grapes on the balcony, where he was playing. He left the remaining few on the plate and forgot about them.

For the next few days, the scorching summer Sun made them shrivel a little more than the day before. Gary noticed this process and decided to see what would happen.

One day, when Gary went to check on the grapes, he found raisins instead! When he showed them to his mother, she laughed.

"I'm glad you've learnt how raisins are made," she said. "But you're lucky the ants didn't take them away!"

23. The Big Piece of Cheese

The ants loved to raid Pat's house for food. He would always leave food lying about, which made it very easy for them. One day, Pat left a huge piece of cheese on the floor. A team of 200 specially trained ants went to get it. They went in stealthily, armed with tiny saws and chisels. One group climbed on the block of cheese and began carving it in half from the top. Another made smaller pieces. A third group arranged them in an orderly line.

Just as they were almost out of the window, the maid came in and saw the long line of ants. She yelped and ran to get a broom. The ants made it out in the nick of time. That night, they ate delicious cheese for dinner!

24. Cleaning out the Attic

Alex's neighbour, Mr. Jackson, was an old man. When he was moving away, Alex decided to help him clean out his attic. When Alex went to his house, Mr. Jackson greeted him warmly. "Please put everything into cartons," he said. "And feel free to look at anything you find interesting." Alex got to work. The attic held fascinating

things. There were old toys, large music boxes and wind-up pocket watches. Then, Alex found the most amazing stamp album. There were stamps from countries all over the world.

Mr. Jackson told Alex about his stamp collection. He let Alex have the album as a token of gratitude for helping him with his cleaning.

25. The Jam Jar

Lola wanted to make a sandwich, but she could not open the jam jar. No matter how much she pulled and twisted, the lid refused to budge. Nobody was at home to help her. Lola thought for a bit. Her mom usually heated the lid on the stove, which got it to loosen up. But she was not allowed to touch the stove by herself. Suddenly, she had an idea. Lola heated some water in the electric kettle and carefully spooned the hot water into a bowl. Then, she turned the jam jar upside-down and let it soak in the hot water.

When she took the jar out, she could open the lid easily! Lola thought it was magic, but it was just science. Metals expand when they are heated and that's how the lid loosened up.

26. The Carnival Roadmap

Heidi and Nash were lost. They had come to the carnival with their school group, but had been separated from them at the popcorn stand. The teachers had instructed them to go and wait at the ticket counter if they got lost.

Heidi and Nash asked the balloon seller for directions. He replied, "Go straight to the rollercoaster. From there, make your way to the dashing teacups. Hop onto the toy train. It will drop you off at the banana boat. Look for the statue of the three clowns and walk in the direction that the tallest clown is pointing at. You'll reach straight to the ticket counter."

The kids thanked the balloon seller and began following his instructions. They rode every ride he had mentioned. Heidi was scared of heights, but she still enjoyed riding the rollercoaster. Nash loved the dashing teacups. They finally reached the three clowns and found their way to the ticket counter.

The bus driver was waiting there. He called their teacher and informed her that they were safe.

41

FEBRUARY

27. The Dare

Troy's friends had dared him to climb on top of a tree and steal an egg from the nest, but he didn't want to do it. "If you're a coward, you can just say so," they teased. But Troy was not scared. He just didn't want to steal the mother bird's egg.

Troy took off his shoes and began climbing. He went higher and higher, until his friends looked like small animals below him. When he reached the nest, Troy did not take an egg. He simply took a twig from the nest and climbed back down.

His friends were impressed with his climbing skills and were happy that he didn't take the egg. Only after he had started climbing did they realise how foolish the dare was.

42

28. Fun Fishing

Grace and her aunt went fishing in the river. Grace thought it was so boring! All they did was sit still with their fishing rods, waiting for the fish to bite. They couldn't even make noise or else they'd scare the fish away. However, they did end up catching a few fish. "At least we'll have fried fish for lunch!" said Grace happily.

Grace's aunt took the fish to the kitchen to gut, clean and cook. Suddenly, Grace heard her aunt gasp! She rushed to see what the matter was. Inside the stomach of the fish she had gutted open, there lay a fat gold coin! It had ancient inscriptions on it. Grace's aunt said it was worth a lot of money.

"Fishing is not so boring after all!" exclaimed Grace.

1. Playing Detective

Jeremy, the innkeeper's son, loved to play detective. He would keep a tab on all the guests at the inn. If they were even vaguely suspicious, Jeremy would be convinced that they were criminals.

One day, a tourist came to stay at the village inn. He was quiet, serious-looking and minded his own business. Naturally, he became Jeremy's newest target. He decided to follow the stranger and see where he went.

The next day, Jeremy shadowed the man all the way to the village square. The man just sat down on a bench and began to look around, taking pictures. Jeremy sat down on another bench and kept an eye on the man. Soon, his eyelids grew heavy. Before he knew it, he had fallen fast asleep. When Jeremy woke up, he was back at the inn. The man he was following had noticed him and carried him back home. Jeremy went to thank him and that's when he learnt that the tourist was actually an architect. He had been hired to remodel some of the village buildings.

Jeremy realised that not all quiet people are fishy!

43

2. Traffic Police Ghost

The ghost of Tinyville was very misunderstood. He was always trying to help the people. But whenever he went to talk to anyone, they ran away! Everyone was afraid of him.

One day, the Tinyville road was being repaired. The workers dug a big hole in the middle of the road and forgot to put up a warning sign. Seeing this, the ghost of Tinyville was very concerned. What if someone fell inside at night? He decided that he must warn people not to take the road.

He stood near the hole that night and whenever he saw someone going towards the road, he would point them in the opposite direction. But everyone got so scared when they saw him, they would always run away and fall straight into the pit!

The ghost was very sad because nobody was listening to him. Then, he had an idea. The following day, he pointed in the direction of the pothole. Everyone went in the other direction as fast as they could! Nobody realised that the ghost was helping them. But the ghost was happy that nobody was falling into the pit.

3. The Bus Scare

Rhea and Rose were travelling long-distance by bus. Along the way, the bus stopped at a petrol station. Rhea and Rose got off to use the washroom. When they returned, their bus was gone! They could not even see any of their fellow passengers around. The girls started to panic. "What will we do?" asked Rose. "Our luggage, phones and money are in the bus!"

Just then, they saw their bus draw up to its place once more. They ran towards it and hopped on. "Where did you go?" Rhea asked the bus driver. "Ma'am," said the driver, "I just took a U-turn since we had to take the opposite route."
The sisters breathed a sigh of relief and took their seats.

4. The Bug Gets a Ride

When the little bug fell asleep on a soft, furry rug, it didn't know that it was actually sleeping on Rocky the puppy. Suddenly, the bug felt the ground moving. It woke up with a jerk. Rocky had woken up from his nap and was running around the house.

The bug felt like he was riding a bull at the rodeo! It held on tight with great difficulty. At one point, the bug almost flew off Rocky's back! Finally, Rocky stopped and the bug slid off his back. It was the craziest ride it had ever been on.

5. The Other Trail

Bryan and Joe were very excited for the school camping trip. When they reached, they were given a map and were strictly instructed not to go off the marked trails.

They agreed and began trekking up one of the trails. After a while, they came to a fork in the path. Instead of going right as the map said, they went left. This trail was uneven and difficult to follow. Just when they were about to turn back, they came upon an abandoned cabin. It was covered with creepers, cobwebs and dust. The boys raced back to tell their teachers. They found out that it was used by bear hunters over a century ago. The boys had chanced upon something very valuable, but they were also scolded for not following the map.

46

6. Ghastly Lessons

Brad and his friends wanted to know if ghosts really existed. They decided to visit a graveyard. That night, they crept out of their beds without telling their parents. When they reached the graveyard, everything was quiet. Suddenly, they heard a wailing sound. A moment later, they saw a white shape floating towards them. Brad and his friends dropped their flashlights and ran for their lives. When the children had gone, the wailing stopped. The white shape started shaking with laughter! It was actually Brad's mother who was dressed as the ghost. His father was making the wailing sound. They wanted to teach the kids a lesson for sneaking out at night.

7. The Little Liar

There was once a girl named Kelly who always lied. One day, a witch asked Kelly for directions to the market. But Kelly gave her the wrong directions. The angry witch placed a curse on Kelly. "Every time you lie, you will lose something," she said. Kelly paid no heed to her. When she went home that day, she lied to her mother about finishing her homework. Immediately, the teddy bear she was holding disappeared. In this manner, she lost a lot of things she loved.

Finally, Kelly could take it no longer. She went to the witch's house and pleaded with her to restore her things. The witch promised her that all her things would come back if she behaved well.

8. The Special Song

For his final project, the young wizard Barry had to create a special song that had the power to cure an illness. He read all the song books in the library. He spoke to all the animals in the forest. He even asked the wild fairies. Nobody could help him. Barry was two days away from the deadline and he had nothing to submit. He was so upset that he got a fever. As he lay in bed, his mother came and sat beside him. She stroked his hair and sang him a lullaby.

Barry felt better instantly. That gave him an idea—it was a mother's lullaby that could cure illnesses! He finally had an answer to his project.

9. The Egret

Every monsoon, a large flock of white egrets would come to Amy's city. They would fly away after the rains would pass. One such season, Amy found an egret with a hurt wing. She gently nursed it back to health. By the end of the season, the egret flew back to its flock.

Just before it was leaving, the egret flew to Amy's window. She tied a little note to its leg. It said: "Hello. This little egret had a broken wing. I have spent the past few months tending to him. His wing is still healing. If anyone gets a hold of him, please treat him gently. I have written my name and address below. Please get in touch if you have any questions. Thank you."

A few weeks later, Amy got a letter from an international society that dealt with animal conservation. They had found the egret and her note. They offered her a chance to visit their organisation in the summer to study endangered species! Amy saved the egret's life and in return, he gave her a summer of adventure.

10. The Ghost in the Village

There was a big old tree right in the centre of the village road. During the day, travellers were grateful for its shade. But at night, the same leafy branches blocked the moonlight and caused a problem.

One night, two boys were walking on the road. As they approached the tree, they saw a white shape floating on it. It was making strange sounds. "Gh-ghost!" yelled the boys, running for their lives. But when the villagers went to check it out the next day, there was no ghost.

They decided to see if they could catch the ghost at night. That night, surely enough, the white shape floated in and settled on the tree. The villagers quickly threw a net on it. They dragged the ghost down and saw that it was no ghost at all! It was just a sheet of white plastic attached to the leg of a crow with a wire. Every night, the crow would come back to its nest in the tree and cry in pain because the wire was hurting it. They untied the crow and set it free. That was the last they saw the ghost!

49

11. Setting a Trap

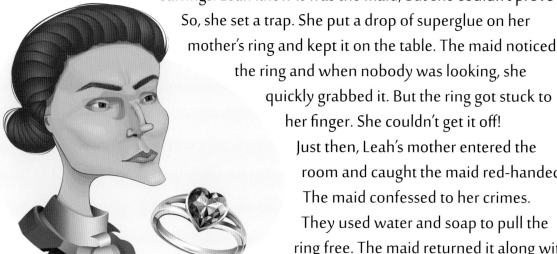

Leah's mother had appointed a new maid. One day, Leah noticed her stealing money from her grandmother's room. A few days later, the maid stole a pair of her mother's earrings. Leah knew it was the maid, but she couldn't prove it. So, she set a trap. She put a drop of superglue on her mother's ring and kept it on the table. The maid noticed the ring and when nobody was looking, she quickly grabbed it. But the ring got stuck to her finger. She couldn't get it off! Just then, Leah's mother entered the room and caught the maid red-handed. The maid confessed to her crimes. They used water and soap to pull the ring free. The maid returned it along with all the other things she had stolen.

12. The Kung Fu Master

Nikko dreamt of becoming a great Kung Fu master one day. So, he wrote to the best master in China, requesting to be his student. The master replied saying that Nikko would have to wrestle a bear to prove his worth. When Nikko read the letter, he was petrified! He did not know how to fight bears. So, he came up with a plan. He wrote to the master saying that he would fight the bear on the coldest day of winter. On that day, Nikko travelled to the master's cabin. "Master," he said, bowing low. "I am ready to fight the bear." The master smiled. "Clever boy!" he said. "We both know that bears hibernate in winter. Because of your intelligence, I will accept you as a student."

13. Treasure Hunt

On the morning of his birthday, Andy woke up to find a note under his pillow. It read, "Dear Birthday Boy, we know you love treasure hunts. So this year, you can have a treasure hunt to find your gifts! Here's your first clue: Look where the monsters stay during the day."

Andy leaped up from bed, excited. He knew that the monsters slept under his bed! When he looked down, there were no monsters, but a big present! He tore open the packaging and found a model airplane. On top of the box was the second clue. It read: "We are hiding under your father's breakfast buddy."

This was a tough one. Andy thought for a while and an idea struck him. He ran down to the kitchen and looked under the pile of newspapers. There, he found two story books. The last clue said, "Come to the place you call your second home."

Andy quickly understood what this meant. He ran to his tree house, where he saw his parents and friends waiting with a big pile of gifts and a huge cake. It was Andy's best birthday!

14. Bonnie's Special Ice Cream

Bonnie loved ice cream. When her school had a cooking competition, it was no surprise that she decided to make ice-cream. But she didn't know where to start!

"You should ask people what they like to eat," advised her mother.

Bonnie asked everyone in the neighbourhood what they liked to eat. Someone said meatloaf. Another person said rabbit stew. Someone else said fried eggs! By the end of the day, Bonnie had a long list of ideas. She picked the ones she liked the most and went shopping with her mother.

They picked up coconut shavings, mango jam and crushed cashew nuts. They also got tubs of strawberry, butterscotch and chocolate ice cream. Bonnie blended the ingredients together and created her first prize-winning ice cream.

15. April and Peach

April had gone on vacation and left her favourite doll, Peach, at home. Peach was very lonely in the cupboard. She thought that April had abandoned her forever. Saddened by this thought, she decided to go back to Toyland.

When April returned home, she could not find Peach anywhere. She became very upset. The other toys decided to help April find Peach. So April, along with Mr. Teddy, hopped on the toy train and went to Toyland.

It was a strange route! They went through a tunnel of pasta, up the trunk of a lollipop tree and down a rabbit hole. Finally, they reached Toyland. April found Peach sitting sadly in her dollhouse. April hugged Peach and promised never to leave her alone again.

16. Riding the Butterfly

Archie the ant had a broken leg. He could not go very far from the anthill.

One day, he saw a beautiful blue butterfly sitting prettily on a rose. Archie looked at her longingly. "What beautiful wings you have!" he said. "You can fly wherever you want." The butterfly smiled. "Would you like a ride?" she asked.

Archie nodded happily and climbed on the butterfly's wing. She floated up and took him for the ride of his life. They flitted above the roses, tulips, sunflowers and dahlias. It seemed as if they were sailing over a riot of colours! Next, the butterfly took Archie to see the animals in the farm. Archie saw fleecy sheep, handsome horses and ambling cows.

The butterfly then told Archie to hold on tight. Archie leaned in excitedly and held on. The butterfly spun round and round! She went upside-down, zoomed sideways and did back flips in the air. She swooped between the horns of a bull and flitted along a cow's back. Archie was giddy with excitement. It was his best ride ever!

17. The Market of Thieves

Alice's summer assignment was to write about the most exciting place in her city. She couldn't think of any such place! So, Alice's father took her to the market of thieves. The market of thieves sold everything you could

possibly think of. Along one lane, they saw shops that had spare parts for vehicles. The next lane had antiques from ancient temples. Another lane had textiles from all over the world. Alice's favourite lane was the one that sold animals. She was sad to see them in cages, but it was the first time she saw animals like sea horses and toucans. By the time Alice came home, she had an exciting place to write about.

18. Blue Tongues

The boys at the boarding school were notorious for stealing sweets from the pantry at night. The teachers tried to catch them, but they were never able to.

One night, the boys decided to steal sweets again. They waited until everyone had gone to sleep. Then, they tiptoed down the stairs. They ran past the teachers' quarters and climbed into the pantry through the window. The boys picked up the first sweets they saw. That night, it happened to be a jar of blue lozenges. They hurried back to the dormitory and polished off the sweets between them. In the dark, they didn't notice that their tongues had turned bright blue! Next morning, when they went to class, all their tongues were blue. They had raided the pantry successfully, but this time they got caught!

19. Collecting Nectar

The first time a bee goes nectar-collecting is a big occasion. On her first day, Bella was very excited. The bees were instructed to stay together at all times.

Bella and her friends set to work in the garden outside the hive. After some time, Bella spotted a bush with yellow flowers. "The nectar from that plant must be delicious!" said Bella, as she flew towards it. As Bella neared the bush, she saw that it had yellow leaves and not flowers. She felt really stupid for flying that far. When she returned, she found that her friends were looking for her. Bella had troubled them for nothing!

55

20. Pickling Limes

Enid bought a dozen limes from the market. When she got home, she left them out on the porch and forgot all about them.

The limes began talking among themselves. "Do you think we'll be made into juice?" asked one. "Maybe we'll be put in some beauty potion," said another. But after waiting for days in the hot sunlight, nothing happened to them.

One day, Enid and her mother saw the limes outside. "Oh no!" said Enid. "They are ruined!"

"No, they are not," replied her mother. "Why don't we pickle them?"

Enid agreed and helped her mother pickle the limes. They were delicious!

21. Battling the Big One

In the olden days, when men still lived in caves, there was a mean mammoth called Bigbully. He would go into everyone's caves and steal their things. One day, Bigbully stole little Oog's stone action figures.

Oog marched up to Bigbully. "Come out and fight!" he screamed. Bigbully saw Oog and laughed. He lowered his head and charged at Oog. But Oog didn't run away. He picked up a sharp rock and jumped on Bigbully's head. Then, he began hitting the mammoth with the rock. With Oog on his head, Bigbully charged towards a tree. But Oog jumped off just in time! Bigbully dashed his head into the tree. Oog took his toys and marched off. Bigbully sat there crying and decided never to steal again.

56

22. The Lost Diamond

The Black Lotus gang had struck again! This time, they had stolen the precious red diamond from the city museum. A group of young students decided to get it back. They found out where the Black Lotus hide out was and went there disguised as wealthy buyers. "We want to buy this diamond," they said and took it in their hands.

"Leave the money in the dumpster on Emerald Street," replied the leader of Black Lotus. "Our men will pick it up at 3 in the morning. Then we will send you the diamond."

Just when he was about to take the diamond back, the students replaced it with a fake one. By the time the criminals realised what had happened, the diamond was already back in the museum.

23. The Pot of Gold

One day, Patty the leprechaun was guarding a pot of gold. It was at the bottom of a rather tall rainbow. As Patty stood guard, he saw a naughty elf climbing up the other end of the rainbow. Patty sighed. It was just another thief coming to steal gold. Patty threw a pail of water at the elf, so that he would lose his balance. But the elf held on tightly and did not slip off. Next, Patty rolled a handful of marbles so that the elf would skid. But the elf dodged all the marbles skilfully! Finally, Patty poured a jug of oil down the rainbow. The elf almost slipped and fell, but held on at the last moment. He climbed up and slid down until he made it to where Patty was standing.

Patty was a strong leprechaun. He could have easily fought off the little elf. But Patty was so impressed with the elf's perseverance, that he gave him a gold coin and let him go free.

57

24. Buried Treasure

Norah's home in the village was being torn down. It had been owned by Norah's family for many generations and she was sad to see it go.

After the house had been demolished, Norah went back to visit the spot. She spotted something shining on the ground and picked it up. It was a large ruby! Excited, Norah hurried to show it to her father.

Father had an explanation. "According to the ancient customs," he said, "it was necessary to bury five precious gems in the ground below any new house. If you keep looking, you will also find an emerald, a diamond, a sapphire and a topaz."

Norah took a spade and dug every day. At first, she only found pieces of broken pottery and clay toys. But after days of digging, she found all the gems. When Norah showed the pottery, clay toys and precious stones to the elders, they were thrilled! The clay toys were bought by a museum and Norah's family were allowed to keep their ancestral jewels.

25. Up in the Sky

After intensive training, it was time for Eric to paraglide for the first time. He put on his harness and stood at the starting point. When the winds were right, Eric got the go-ahead signal.

He opened his chute and started sprinting. In a few seconds, the winds lifted him up into the sky. Eric glided over the fields and the lakes, which looked tiny from above. He felt like a bird! After a while, he tugged the lines to his left and right, and landed on a field of tulips. Eric caught his breath. What a thrilling experience!

26. In the Pyramid

Ryan's parents were archaeologists. They took Ryan with them when they went to work around the Egyptian pyramids, but he found it very boring. He would loiter around aimlessly, looking for ways to amuse himself.

One day, Ryan wandered into one of the pyramids. As he ran his hands over the lid of the Pharaoh's coffin, he felt a bump at one spot. He pushed it and the bricks on one wall shifted to reveal a room! Ryan was scared, but he went inside. The room was filled with treasure that had been buried with the Pharaoh.

Ryan ran to tell his parents about his find. It turned out that it had been what they were searching for all along! Thanks to Ryan, they had found the Pharaoh's lost treasure.

27. Riding the Sand Dunes

As Savannah rode to the desert in the car, she was very excited. She was going to ride a camel! Savannah loved the desert. The beautiful sand dunes looked like a golden sea. The camel was very tall, even when it was sitting down. Savannah had to be helped on to its back. The camel was very gentle. Riding on its back, Savannah felt as if she was bobbing on a wave. Just as she got off the camel, the winds began to blow really fast. There was a sandstorm coming. Savannah and her parents got into the car and waited until the storm settled. When they came out, the shapes of the dunes had completely changed! It was like being in a whole new desert.

60

28. On the Movie Set

Mark's uncle was a movie director. One day, he was filming in a zoo and invited Mark along. The movie was about a bunch of naughty monkeys. Mark was having a great time watching how the movie was being made. But then, he noticed that the toffees in his pocket kept vanishing. Mark buttoned his pocket so that they would not fall out. But when he looked again, the button was undone and more toffees had gone!

Mark found a small mousetrap on the movie set. He put it in his pocket along with the toffees. A while later, he heard a small yelp and saw a finger stuck in the mousetrap. It was one of the monkeys starring in the movie! Mark had a good laugh at the monkey's expense.

29. The Imaginary Friends

Many children have imaginary friends. But when they grow older, they stop playing with their imaginary friends. The poor imaginary friends have nowhere to go. So a caravan comes to take them away. They all live in the caravan and look for other abandoned imaginary friends.

One night, the caravan broke down in a deserted place. After looking around, they found a small building. The place was a home for the elderly. The nurse called them in and gave them place to rest for the night. The next morning, when the elderly people came down for breakfast, they saw all their old imaginary friends! They were glad to see them and asked them to stay back. Everyone was happy.

61

30. Sea Breeze

Sea Breeze, the young racehorse, was sure that he would lose the race one day. He was new to horse-racing and lacked confidence. But he decided to try his best. When the gates opened, Sea Breeze ran very fast. A horse named Giddyup was racing right in front of him. Sea Breeze galloped harder, but he couldn't reach Giddyup. Just moments before the finish line, Sea Breeze tripped on a stone. He stumbled into the finish line at top speed, with Giddyup right besides him.

It was a very close finish and nobody knew who had won. At last, the winner was announced. It was Sea Breeze! He had won by a whisker. Sea Breeze won a shiny medal and also found new confidence.

31. The Girl Who Threw Stones

June always threw stones at birds, laughing when they would get hurt. Everyone told her that it was cruel, but she just would not listen. To teach her a lesson, a witch cast a spell on her. She turned June into a little blue bird!

When June looked into the mirror, she was shocked. But then she got excited. She could fly! June flew outside her room and sat on a tree. The moment she sat down, stones went flying at her. She saw that some kids were trying to hit her with their slingshots. June flew into a bush for cover. But there, a monkey searching for fruit began pinching her. June saw some other birds and decided to sit with them. But they shooed her away because they knew she was the girl who had thrown stones at them. June was tired. Everywhere she went, she was targeted and troubled. In the end, she curled up under a car and slept. When she woke up, she was a girl again. But she was a changed person. From then on, June was never mean to anybody—animal or human! She always tried to protect all the birds and animals around her.

62

1. At the Beach

There was once a crab that lived on the seashore. He had big dreams of living in a castle of his own. "If you want a castle, why don't you build it here, under the sea?" asked his mother. But the crab was very lazy. "I'm royalty," he would say. "I can't build my own castle!"

One summer afternoon, the crab scuttled onto the beach and saw a large sand castle. He went inside and made himself comfortable. "This is going to be my castle!" he said gleefully. The crab closed his eyes and decided to take a nap.

Suddenly, he heard the sound of human voices. He opened his eyes to see a child and his father looking at him. "Can we cook him, daddy?" asked the little boy. "Hmm, maybe," replied the man, stroking his chin.

As soon as the crab heard this, he burrowed under the sand and scuttled away as fast as he could. He didn't want to be eaten! He went under the sea and built his own house. Never again was he going to take anything that he didn't earn!

2. The Dreamcatcher

Simon used to have a lot of nightmares. One day, his mother hung a dreamcatcher above his head. "This is a dreamcatcher," she said. "It will catch all your bad dreams in this net and not let them reach you."

That night, Simon slept soundly. But the dreamcatcher was having an exciting time!

A scary nightmare about a child-eating monster was trying to go past it. The dreamcatcher fought hard against it. But the nightmare was very strong and kept fighting back. Then, another dream came along. It was about a big, angry dinosaur. The dreamcatcher caught the monster dream and fed it to the dinosaur in the other dream. This made the dinosaur happy. The dream changed to a happy one about a dinosaur playing football.

3. Science Lab Experiment

Justine thought that the science laboratory was the most exciting place in the whole school. She was too young to go in, but she liked to watch the older kids wear gloves and perform experiments. One day, when no one was in the laboratory, Justine went inside. She thought it would be harmless to play with the liquids. She mixed the blue one into the green one and put in a bit of pink salt. When she added a yellow powder to the mixture, it started bubbling and caused a small explosion. Justine's face turned black with smoke and she stood stunned. She ran out of the laboratory and decided to not enter until she was old enough to understand it.

4. Snowball and His New Friend

Snowball was a white kitten that loved falling asleep in snug corners. One day, Snowball spotted a van outside his house. He jumped into it and curled up on the soft seat. Soon, Snowball fell asleep.

When he awoke, he saw that the van was moving. Snowball looked out of the window anxiously. The van seemed to be going on a familiar route. They were going to the vet! Snowball whimpered softly and hid under the seat.

The van came to a stop, but nobody came to get Snowball. Finally, he heard the door open. But the driver just put something heavy near Snowball and went back out. He then started to drive away.

When Snowball peeked out from underneath the seat, he saw that the heavy thing was actually a little goat! It was being sent to live with Snowball and his family. Snowball told the goat all about the people who lived in his house. By the time they reached home, Snowball had a new friend. They had a lot of fun together.

5. The Little Lamp

The little lamp sat quietly in the corner of the table. Ever since electricity came to the village, no one used lamps. The lamp felt sad and unloved. It ran away from home.

Even outside, nobody had any use for it. The lamp sat under a tree and waited for a miracle. Soon, it dozed off to sleep. When it woke up, it saw a big genie looking at it! "Little lamp," said the genie kindly. "I don't have a home. If you don't mind, may I live inside you?"

The little lamp was overjoyed. "Yes, of course!" it replied. "Nobody needs me for anything these days." The genie moved his things into the lamp and made a lovely home inside. Together, they travelled the world and granted lots of wishes.

66

6. The Doorbell

A bunch of naughty neighbourhood children loved to trouble old Mr. and Mrs. Jones. They would ring their doorbell and run off before anyone could open the door.

So, the old couple decided to teach the kids a lesson. Mrs. Jones had an idea. One morning, she sprinkled some itching powder on the doorbell. As usual, the kids rang the bell and ran off. The Joneses just smiled and waited.

The next day, the kids came back and rang the bell. But this time, they waited till the door was opened. They apologised for their bad behaviour and showed Mr. and Mrs. Jones their red, itchy palms.

Mrs. Jones gave them a special medicine for their hands. Since that day, the kids and the Joneses became friends.

7. The New Bus Driver

The school bus had a new driver. He didn't know the way to school. All the kids tried to give him directions, but they, too, were not sure. The bus went round and round. Finally, they took a turn that seemed right.

But instead of reaching school, they reached the zoo!

To their surprise, they saw their teacher standing outside the zoo. She laughed when she heard what had happened. "We were supposed to come to the zoo for a visit anyway," she said. "So it's good that you reached here, even if you came by mistake!"

The kids spent a nice day at the zoo and their teacher gave the new driver the correct directions to drive back to school.

8. The Cure for All Diseases

In a village far away, there lived an old woman who was rumoured to have a cure for all diseases. Arnold did not believe it. He decided to go and see for himself.

He walked through many forests and crossed many rivers, until he finally reached her house. The old lady smiled at Arnold and invited him to sit beside her.

"Do you really have the cure for all diseases?" he asked her. The old woman beckoned him to come closer. "I'm no doctor," she whispered. "But I have a cure that generally works. Would you like to know what it is?" Arnold nodded eagerly.

"Nothing works like a good joke!" she exclaimed. "Make people shake with laughter and they get better in no time."

9. A New Hobby for the Village Ghost

The village ghost thought he was the finest singer in the world. But actually, he was a very bad singer! Every night, when the villagers were trying to sleep, he would sing on the top of his voice and disturb everyone.

The villagers decided to help him get a new hobby. First, they asked him to try ice skating. But the ghost just slipped all over the ice and hurt himself. What's more, he bumped into all the kids and made them slip as well. Next, the ghost tried painting. But all he did was make a mess! And it wasn't even an artistic mess. The ghost tried many more things, but they all had similar results. Finally, he went to the village priest and asked for a suggestion.

"Why don't you find a hobby that helps the villagers?" the priest suggested. "You can knit blankets and sweaters for us!" The ghost liked this idea. Surprisingly, he picked up knitting very quickly. If you visit the village today, you will still see the ghost knitting sweaters and scarves for the villagers.

10. The Stream

A small stream trickled down the mountainside. She was content, but she wanted to travel beyond the mountains. The stream had heard stories of mighty rivers and gushing waterfalls from the birds and animals that came to her for a drink of water. So, she set out into the world along with the fish she carried with her. They rode over rocks and gushed past flat lands. The little stream kept getting fatter and more fish started living with her. Even boats started riding in her waters. But she still felt very ordinary. She thought she would never be a fabled river or waterfall.

One day, the fat stream came across a high and jagged wall of rock. She planned to stop there and become a lake. But she was a curious one. She decided to look over the rocks. Before she knew it, she lost her balance and tumbled downwards!

To her surprise, she was completely okay. That's when she realised that she had stopped being a stream a long time ago. She had become a river and was now a mighty waterfall.

69

11. On Mars

Zee the robot didn't like his job. He was made to do silly things like dig the ground or pick fruits. He was in such a bad state of mind, that he thought he should just push the self-destruct button. Somehow, he decided against it.

One day, Zee was launched off into space and sent to Mars. His mission was to detect any life forms and collect samples of the rocks on Mars. Zee felt very important now. He roamed all over Mars, digging the ground and looking for signs of life. Every day, he would send reports back home. Zee realised that his old 'job' was only practice for his mission. He was glad he didn't self-destruct!

12. The Special Horn

Gallop wanted to be a unicorn with all her heart. One night, she ran away from the stables in search of the last living unicorn. On her way, she helped a farmer plough his field. He gave her a warm shawl in return. She also helped a little boy reach school on time and, in return, he gave her a pencil. At last, after days of travelling, she came to a place deep within the forest. There, the last living unicorn was waiting.

"How can I get a horn and become a unicorn?" asked Gallop. The old unicorn smiled. "The horn is made from the rewards for your good deeds," he said. Gallop then gave him all the gifts she had been given along the way. The old unicorn magically turned them into one horn. Gallop was now a unicorn!

13. Digging to China

Molly the mole had heard that if you dug straight into the ground, you would emerge from the opposite side. Molly wanted to dig her way to China and see the moles who lived there. So, she started digging. Within a few hours, she had already reached a surface. "That was quick," she thought, popping her head through the hole. There were Chinese people and buildings everywhere. Molly had reached China! The little mole looked around for a while. But she missed home. So Molly went back down her hole and emerged from the other side, back home. Molly thought she went to China, but what she had seen was actually a Chinese village 10 minutes away from her house!

14. Attacking Earth

Aliens from the planet of Eevul wanted to take over Earth. Before they could launch an attack, they sent four aliens to find to what Earth was like.

When the aliens went back, each of them gave a report.

The first had landed in a desert. He said, "Earth is boring. There's only sand everywhere."

The second alien had landed in the monkey enclosure of a zoo. "Earth is a dangerous place," he said. "It's filled with strange pick-pockets". The third, who had landed in a volcano, said that Earth was very hot and dangerous. The last one had landed on the tip of an iceberg. He said, "Earth is just a block of ice!"

The aliens were dumbfounded! "Earth must be full of strange magic," they said. "We better not mess with it."

15. The Secret Circus

The secret circus was a magical place. But only good children were allowed to see it. Louis and Rachel were good children. They would help their mother, do their homework and were well-behaved. One day, Rachel and Louis received an invitation in their mail, to visit the circus. They were very excited and wore their best clothes. When they reached the circus, they were greeted by a dancing baby elephant! "Welcome to the secret circus! I will be your guide for today." it said.

Rachel and Louis followed the elephant around and saw different sights. They saw dancing fish, a horse that ate fire and blew clouds of smoke from its nose, a lion that did card tricks and a mirror that showed you any place in the world.

At last, the elephant took them to a little tent. The kids were given wands and allowed to try their own magic tricks. Louis swished his wand and made a cake appear out of thin air. Rachel made a teapot sing! They had a wonderful time.

16. Following the Scent

The coffee estate was huge and very beautiful. It was full of coffee plants hanging with clumps of luscious berries. Surrounding the plants were tall trees that gave them shade. Nina was visiting the estate with her family. She had started chasing a little butterfly and got lost. Now, she was standing amidst the coffee plants with her family nowhere in sight. The smell of delicious, freshly brewed coffee reached her. Nina forgot all about being lost and started following the scent.

She reached a small garden set up for brewing and tasting coffee. To her relief, her family was there! They were so happy to see her. Nina told her family how the scent of coffee helped her find them.

17. Escape

There was a small goldfish named Coral who lived in the coral reef. One day, someone fished her out and put her in a public aquarium. Coral was not happy. She didn't like swimming in circles while people stared at her. She wanted to go back to the sea.

A little child named Ross came to her tank. "You look really sad," he said to Coral. "Do you want help?" Coral asked him to take her back to the sea. When nobody was around, Ross opened his water bottle and scooped Coral in. He kept the bottle upright in his jacket.

At the exit, the guard searched Ross's bag. But he didn't check his jacket! Ross was able to take Coral out safely. He took her to the closest beach and set her free.

18. The Enchanted Sweets

The owner of the sweet shop was tired of having his sweets stolen by the naughty village children. He put a spell on the sweets and sat back to watch the fun.

As soon as the kids put the stolen sweets on their tongues, something strange happened. Every time they tried to speak, all they could say was, "I'm a naughty child and I like to steal sweets!"

They said it to their friends, their teachers and everyone they tried speaking to. Once the kids noticed they were under this strange spell, they stopped speaking. They were quiet all day and finally went to the sweet shop owner. Seeing their sorry faces, the shop owner lifted the spell. No more sweets were stolen after that day.

19. A Lifesaving Ride

Todd had gone deep sea fishing. He had already caught a few fish, but he wanted more. Suddenly, the weather started changing and the sea grew rough. The waves started tossing the boat around and Todd fell overboard. Before he could be hoisted back in, the boat rocked away on a big wave. Todd was stranded in the middle of the sea!

He was struggling to stay afloat. Suddenly, he felt something nudging his leg. Before he knew it, he was on a dolphin! The gentle creature had swum underneath him and taken him on its back.

The dolphin took Todd back to the boat and then swam off. Todd was always grateful to the dolphin that saved his life.

20. The Black Cloud

A fluffy white cloud floated in the sky. For the past few days, she had noticed that she was slowly turning darker. At first, it didn't bother her. "It will probably be fine soon," she thought. But a few weeks later, she became completely black. Nobody could explain why. The cloud began to believe that she was very sick.

The cloud was so sad that she started dropping lower and lower in the sky. As she got closer to Earth, she saw many more black clouds like her. They had also sunk low because they were sad. None of them knew why they had turned black. All of them thought that they were ill.

The clouds hugged each other and began to cry. As they cried, they began to feel lighter and lighter. When they had wrung out all their tears, they floated back up. They were as white as snow again.

The clouds had released their tears and felt happy. But they didn't know that their tears had made the people on Earth very happy, too!

21. The Superhero

Spindly the spider was watching a movie. The story was very interesting. It was about a man who was bitten by a spider. But instead of getting a painful bite mark, he got super powers! That gave Spindly an idea. "If a man bites me," thought Spindly. "Maybe I will become a super-spider!"

Spindly crept into a restaurant and hid under a spoon. His plan was to jump between the person's teeth at the last minute. But the spoon he was clinging to went into a bowl of hot soup! Spindly yelped and jumped out. He tried another spoon.

This spoon went into an ice cream sundae. Spindly almost froze solid! Finally, he got a spoon that went in a nice salad.

Just as Spindly was about to be bitten, the person saw him and screamed. He flung the spoon, along with Spindly, to a dusty corner. In the end, instead of super powers, all Spindly got was a backache. He gave up trying to get bitten after all that.

22. The Donkey Prince

There once lived a prince who was very lazy and selfish. He made everyone else work very hard, but would do nothing himself. The people of the kingdom asked a wizard to teach him a lesson. When the prince woke up the next morning, he saw that he had turned into a donkey. He could no longer command anyone. He had to carry heavy things and run errands all day. No one appreciated his hard work.

The prince realised how unfair he had been. Seeing this, the wizard turned him back into a prince. After that, the prince became a kind, just and very good ruler.

23. The Silly Genie

Rita found an old, dusty lamp while cleaning the attic. When she was rubbing it clean, a genie swirled out! "Your wish is my command," said the genie. "I would like to be a genie for a day!" exclaimed Rita.

The genie snapped her fingers. Immediately, Rita found herself inside a lamp, dressed as a genie. After a while, someone rubbed the lamp. Rita went out to grant some wishes. The person who had rubbed the lamp wished to be very handsome. Rita wasn't sure which spell to use. She ended up turning his skin pink! The next person wished for a car, but she gave him a rocking horse. Rita kept granting silly wishes all day. She had a good time, but the wishers did not!

24. The Green Bags

Emily was tired from her flight and couldn't wait to get home. She picked up her suitcase from the baggage conveyor and left the airport. When she reached home and opened her suitcase, she was shocked.

She had taken someone else's suitcase by mistake! Emily searched for a name or phone number, but couldn't find anything. She thought that she would never get her things back. Just then, her phone rang. It was the owner of the green bag. Thankfully, Emily had left her details on her own suitcase. They exchanged suitcases and were glad that at least one of them had left their contact details on the bag.

78

25. Video Game Land

For her birthday, Ivy's toys decided to take her on a magical train ride. That night, when everyone was asleep, they woke Ivy up and took her to the magic train.

"The magic train goes to a new place every day," explained the teddy bear. "Let's see where we go today!"

To their pleasant surprise, the train stopped at a station called Video Game Land. It was the world in which all the video game characters stayed. Ivy took their autographs and they promised to help her win all the games she played. Ever since that day, Ivy became a champion at video games. It was the best birthday gift ever!

26. The Blue Girl

Carrie was strictly instructed to not enter her father's study. Her father was a scientist working on a top-secret project and not even her mother was allowed to go inside. But Carrie was a very curious girl. One morning, when she was on her way to breakfast, she saw that the door to her father's study was wide open. Her father was nowhere to be seen, so Carrie sneaked inside.

In the study was a machine with many knobs and buttons. When Carrie pushed a button, a ray shot out of the machine and hit her in the face! Immediately, Carrie started turning blue. She ran to her room and looked at the mirror. Her skin was completely blue!

Carrie hid under the bed, very embarrassed. Eventually, her father found her there. "You'll stay blue for a whole day now," said her father. "You have to go to school like this!"

At school, everyone stared at Carrie. When they asked her how she turned blue, she told them she had eaten too many blueberries. She couldn't wait to turn normal again!

79

27. Stinky Peggy

Peggy the cat loved to jump into buckets and tunnels. One day, she went on a picnic with her class. When they reached the picnic spot, Peggy spotted a bucket and jumped

right in. Only once she was inside, did she realise that it was not a bucket, but a stinky garbage bin. Peggy jumped out and went crying to her teacher. Just then, a group of foxes spotted the cats and came to attack them. They could see all their delicious food and they wanted some, too! But when they got a whiff of Peggy, she smelled so bad that the foxes held their breath and ran away.

Everyone thanked Peggy for driving away the foxes. They all gave her a hug—but only after she had taken a good, long bath!

28. The Stars that Forgot to Twinkle

One afternoon, hundreds of years ago, the stars had a party. They danced and sang to their hearts' content. By the end of the party, some of them were so tired that they

fell fast asleep and forgot to twinkle at night. The sailors on one particular ship looked up at the sky and were confused. The stars were missing! They could not see the familiar patterns in the sky. Their sense of direction was completely mixed up. That night, the sailors ended up taking a lot of wrong turns. They reached a completely unfamiliar place. By morning, they realised that they had discovered a whole new continent! The sailors thanked the stars for what had happened!

29. The Travelling Tree

Ever since it was a seed, the oak tree wanted to be different. It didn't want to take root in the old forest. It wanted to go somewhere exciting.

When it was finally time for it to take root, the oak tree went to the wise old tortoise and asked him for advice. "Why don't you hop on my back?" said the tortoise "I'm going to travel across the sea. If you see any island you like, you can take root." The oak tree travelled the seas on the back of the old tortoise, until the day they spotted a lovely beach with white sand and coconut trees. The oak tree decided to take root there. To this day, people wonder how it reached there!

81

30. Fighting Fire

Lucy was at home alone, watching television on a Saturday afternoon. Suddenly, she heard someone scream from next door. Lucy ran out and saw that the curtain on her neighbour's kitchen window was on fire.

Lucy acted immediately. She took the thickest blanket from her house and threw it over the curtain. Then, she ran and got the fire extinguisher. She sprayed the extinguisher on the curtain until the fire went out. Except for the scorched curtain, everything in the house was saved.

Her neighbour thanked her for her quick thinking and help. Lucy had quite a story to tell her parents when they got home!

1. The Little Song

A little song was stuck inside a pencil. It couldn't wait to jump out on a piece of paper. However, nothing could be done until someone bought the pencil from the store.

One day, a school girl came into the store and bought the pencil. The song was overjoyed! If she just gave it a chance, it would pour itself on the paper. But sadly, it never got its chance. The girl had many pencils already. This one was only a back-up. During an exam, the girl lent this pencil to her classmate. Again, the song thought that its chance had come. But the boy only used it to draw diagrams. In the end, the classmate forgot to return the pencil to the girl. He took it home and lent it to his brother. By now, the little song had lost hope of ever being written. Little did it know that the classmate's brother was a songwriter in a band!

The songwriter took the pencil and began writing. Out popped the little song onto the piece of paper. It was a lovely song that went on to become very famous.

2. The Floating Island

There was once a tiny island that could not stay in one place. It kept floating around on the waves, going from place to place. The island hated floating. It had no friends, because it floated away before it could get close to anyone.

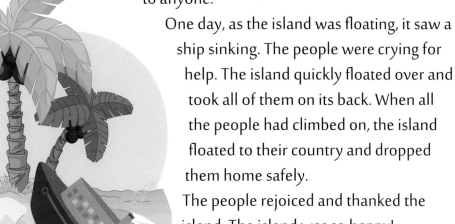

One day, as the island was floating, it saw a ship sinking. The people were crying for help. The island quickly floated over and took all of them on its back. When all the people had climbed on, the island floated to their country and dropped them home safely.

The people rejoiced and thanked the island. The island was so happy! It decided to keep floating around the ocean and help everyone in need.

3. Sleepy Joe

Joe would wake up late every day and go to school in a rush. "This habit of yours will get you in trouble one day," said his mother. But Joe never paid her any heed.

One morning, Joe woke up especially late and ran to get ready. He was still very sleepy while brushing his teeth. He did not notice that instead of using toothpaste, he had squeezed foot cream on his toothbrush.

Joe started brushing and his mouth filled up with a bitter taste. He spat out the foot cream and ran to tell his mother what had happened. She laughed and they both hoped he wouldn't get a stomach ache because of his silly mistake.

4. The Wrong Number

Noah had recently moved into a new house. It was a very nice house, but they would keep getting phone calls asking for the old owner, who was a vet.

Noah would politely inform the callers that the number belonged to someone else. He would also provide them with the vet's new number.

One afternoon, Noah was home alone when the phone rang. He picked it up to hear a crying child on the other end. "Please help," said the sobbing child. "My dog is hurt. I'm home alone." Noah tried to comfort the child. He took down his address, only to realise that he lived only two houses down the road.

Noah called the vet's office immediately. Then, he went to the boy's address and saw that the dog was badly hurt. Noah cleaned the dog's leg while they waited for the ambulance. Soon, it came and took the dog to the vet. When it brought the dog back later that day, it was all bandaged up. But its leg was saved, thanks to Noah's quick action. Because of that incident, Noah, the boy and his dog became good friends.

5. The Shoe Story

One morning, Nathan was in a great hurry to go to the playground. He got dressed in a flash and rushed outside. On the way, his shoes started pinching him. "That's strange," thought Nathan. "I've had these shoes for months. They've never hurt me before." Nathan's feet began to ache. He began to walk funny. This made him trip on the road and he fell down with a loud thump. Sitting on the ground, Nathan got a good look at his shoes. He saw that he had put the left shoe on his right foot and the right shoe on his left foot! Because of his great hurry, Nathan ended up with sore feet!

6. River Rafting

David's parents loved adventure sports. David, however, was scared to try them. His parents never forced him, but always hoped that someday he would overcome his fear and try something new. On one occasion, the family had the chance to go river rafting. Everyone was so excited that David decided to resist his fear and give it a shot. He strapped on a life jacket and took his place on the raft. They even had a trained guide. The raft rode over the gushing river water and within seconds, everyone was completely drenched. Some of the rocky places even scared David's parents. But David was having so much fun, he forgot to feel scared. In the end, David was really happy he had gone river rafting!

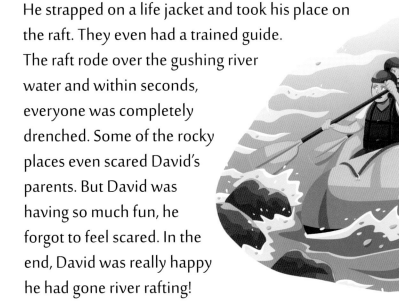

7. The Paper Plane's New Home

The paper plane was tired of flying. It had flown everywhere and had seen everything. Now, it wanted to explore the ocean. But the paper plane knew that it would fall to pieces if its skin touched the water. So, the paper plane asked the glass bottle for help. It entered the bottle and the bottle rolled into the sea. The waves swallowed the bottle to the depths of the ocean. The paper plane met sharks, whales, stingrays and many more underwater creatures. Even the bottle made friends and had a good time.

Eventually, they found an abandoned ship under the sea. The bottle and plane decided to make it their new home. They stayed back under the sea with their new friends and lived happily ever after.

8. Sammy in Skates

Chet the cheetah was bullying the jungle animals. He would take their things and run off with them. Once, he even grabbed Baxter the baboon's toothbrush—while he was using it!

Sammy the antelope wanted to catch Chet and teach him a lesson. But Chet was the fastest runner in the jungle. There was no way Sammy could catch him. Then, he had an idea. He would use roller skates!

But alas, there were no skates available in the jungle.

So, Sammy decided to make his own skates. He bought four bars of slippery soap and tied them to his hooves. With his soapy skates, Sammy caught Chet the cheetah easily and made him return everything.

9. The Singing Clock

There was an old grandfather clock in Phil's house. It needed to be wound every morning to work properly. But this wasn't an ordinary grandfather's clock. It was magical! Not only did it show the time, it also sang loudly to remind people if they had forgotten to do something.

The clock would remind Phil's mother to take her medicines and Phil to finish his homework. One busy morning, the clock began to sing and nobody knew why. Phil's mother had taken her medicines. Phil had done his homework. The dog had been fed.

They wondered if the clock was broken. Just then, Phil's sister perked up. "Aha!" she yelled. "The clock is reminding us to wind it up, or else it won't work!"

She was right. The clock was using its last shreds of energy to sing to them. They wound him up quickly and resumed their work. What an intelligent clock!

10. Bubba the Bear Cub

Bubba the bear cub loved the city. He wanted to live there and leave the forest.

"You can't do that," said his friends. "Humans are scared of bears." But Bubba didn't listen.

He decided to ask Santa for help. He wrote him a letter and mailed it to the North Pole. Bubba also started behaving very well, because only good bears got their wishes.

On Christmas morning, Bubba woke up in a small box. He was confused. But then, a little girl opened the box and hugged him. He had turned into a teddy bear! Now, Bubba lives in the city with his owner. He is happy, but sometimes he wishes he could go back to being a real bear.

11. Trapped in the T.V.

Kim had a bad habit. She would sit right in front of the television, with her nose nearly touching the screen. Her mother warned her that it was bad for her eyes, but Kim never listened. One day, when Kim was watching a show about birds, the T.V. swallowed her! Kim found herself sitting on a branch with the birds. She started to panic. How would she go home? Kim looked up at the sky and saw that it was the television screen. Through it, she could see her living room. That gave her an idea. Kim asked the birds to grab her with their talons. Then, they flew up to the sky and tossed her through the screen. Kim landed safely in her house. She vowed to stop sitting too close to the T.V.

12. Super Grandpa

Cindy's grandpa had come to live with them for a few days. Cindy loved her grandpa. He told her lots of stories and was a very interesting person.

However, Cindy couldn't help but be a little suspicious about him. Each night, Cindy heard noises coming from his room. Sometimes, in the mornings, he seemed very tired, as though he had not slept all night. One night, Cindy decided to investigate the matter. When she heard the noises, she crept out of bed and peeked into her grandpa's room. What Cindy saw gave her a big shock. Her grandpa was putting on a cape and a costume. Then, he flew out the window!

"My grandpa is a superhero!" thought Cindy happily. "And nobody knows about it!" When Grandpa came back, Cindy told him that she knew his secret. "Please keep my secret," said her grandpa. "And in return, I'll take you along on some of my missions." Cindy thought that was a great idea. She agreed to keep her grandpa's secret. What's more, he could now tell her many more stories about his adventures!

13. The Animal Saviour

One night, a robin came to Grandpa's window and alerted him that an evil man was going to cut off the elephant's tusks at the zoo. Cindy climbed into Grandpa's arms and they flew to the zoo. "You can speak to animals?" Cindy asked.

"Yes," Grandpa replied. "Human beings have enough heroes. I am an animal superhero."

When they reached the zoo, they saw the man behind the elephant. "Look out!" screamed Cindy at the top of her voice.

The elephant woke up with a start. It started trumpeting and kicking everything, including the man who had come to steal his tusks! The evil man got kicked in the face and fell down. The zoo authorities called the police, who arrested the evil man. Cindy had saved the day!

90

14. Beach Rescue

One night, Grandpa took Cindy along with him to the beach. The sea gulls had told him that a huge whale had been washed ashore and was unable to go back to the sea. It was too hot for the whale to live on land and it had to go back.

Grandpa tried to haul the whale back into the water himself, but it was too huge.

Then, he had an idea. He turned towards the sea and started whistling a tune.

In no time, a team of dolphins came swimming to the shore. With their help, Grandpa and Cindy pushed the whale back into the sea. They watched the whale and the dolphins swim away happily and went back home.

15. Cindy Takes Over

Even though she couldn't fly or talk to animals like her grandpa, Cindy would try to help animals in whatever way she could. One day at school, she saw a little girl gazing up a tree. "What's the matter?" asked Cindy. The girl pointed to the very top, where a

kitten was hanging from a branch. It was about to fall down. There was no time to even climb up and save it. Cindy thought quickly. She ran to the school gym and grabbed the volleyball net. She asked the little girl to hold one end and she held the other. When the kitten fell down, it plopped into the net, completely unhurt. When Cindy told Grandpa her story, he was very proud of her.

16. Intergalactic Food Fight

This story takes place in the future. It is the year 3030. A spaceship from Earth is patrolling space. Suddenly, they receive a distress call from Planet Hotsauce. Hotsauce is a friendly planet that makes hot sauce for all the planets in the universe. The spaceship stops at Hotsauce and sees that it's being attacked by aliens from Planet Fruitsalad. There is an army of evil strawberries and bananas leading the fight. The spaceship quickly takes its guns out and sprays hot sugar on the fruits. The fighters of Fruitsalad begin to get cooked. They run away from Hotsauce. The Hotsauceans thank the spaceship and give them bottles of extra spicy hot sauce.

17. The Buried Treasure

Tom was on his way to see his grandmother. Suddenly, he remembered something. "Oh, no!" he said. "I've forgotten to get her a gift! What should I do now?"
Tom was walking along, thinking hard about what to do. Suddenly, a parrot flew in front of him. "Hello there!" squawked the bird. "I'm Percy, the pirate parrot!"
He started talking to Tom and told him all about his pirate life. Percy used to steal treasures from wrecked ships and hide them all over the world.
"There's an old cave up that hill," said Percy. "I have a chest of gold coins hidden there. Will you help me dig it out?" Tom was in no hurry, so he agreed to help Percy out.
But when they reached the cave, they found that it was occupied by a big lion!
Tom was worried, but Percy did not seem nervous at all. "Hey lion," squawked Percy.
"They're giving out free hamburgers at the waterfall." As soon as the lion heard this, he ran off to find the burgers. Tom and Percy quickly dug the treasure out. For his help, Percy gave Tom two gold coins. Tom finally had a gift for Granny!

18. What Made Doris Smile

The Frog King and Queen lived under a lovely mushroom near a lake. They were very happy. However, their daughter, Princess Doris, was not. She never smiled, no matter what they tried. They invited doctors, magicians and musicians to make her smile, but they couldn't help her. They even tried to get a human to kiss her! But Doris wouldn't have that. "Ew!" she said, turning up her nose.

In winter, the lake was covered with ice. Many people came to skate on it. One day, Doris saw a little puppy trying to skate. But he kept sliding and slipping! Doris found it really funny. She started laughing loudly. Doris helped the puppy skate. When they were tired, she took it home. Since then, Doris laughed everyday for the rest of her life.

19. Invisible Juice

Craig saw an advertisement on the school notice board. It read: "If you want to volunteer for a fun experiment, come to the chemistry laboratory at 10 a.m." Craig was curious. He decided to go and see what it was about.

When he reached the laboratory, he saw a teacher and a group of senior students. They made Craig drink a sparkling blue liquid. He started turning invisible!

"This is my chance to teach the school bully a lesson!" Craig thought. He went up to the bully and started poking his tummy.

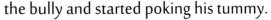

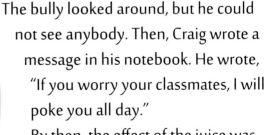

The bully looked around, but he could not see anybody. Then, Craig wrote a message in his notebook. He wrote, "If you worry your classmates, I will poke you all day."

By then, the effect of the juice was wearing off. He ran back to the lab before the bully could catch him.

20. Kidnapped

One day, the sea creatures woke up to see that a monkey had kidnapped the mermaid. He was carrying her up a high mountain. The sea creatures asked the fox to help them. The fox was kind and helpful. He went to the mountain and followed the scent of the mermaid. Soon, he reached a huge cave with a pool deep inside. He was surprised to see the mermaid and monkey splashing happily in the water!

That's when the mermaid told him the full story. The monkey wanted to learn how to swim, but he was embarrassed. So, he had brought the mermaid to the hidden pool inside the cave. After the swimming lesson was over, the fox and monkey took the mermaid back to the sea.

21. Blueberry Party

A little girl was plucking blueberries in a garden. She put them in a pail and went inside for lunch. The blueberries were all bored in the heat of the sun. They decided to have some fun and began singing and dancing heartily. The noise attracted the sugar, salt and fennel, and they also jumped into the pail.

It was very cramped inside the pail and they were packed tightly together. As they danced, they bumped against each other. Finally, they were tired. They slumped against each other, feeling all squishy and soft. But when the sugar, salt and fennel said good-bye and got up to leave, they saw that they were all stuck. They had danced themselves into a blueberry jam!

22. One Superpower

One day, Helen met a genie who agreed to give her a superpower for one hour. Helen chose the power to fly. She flew over the trees, the buildings and the roads. It felt wonderful to be high up in the air. But then, she spotted something shocking.

Helen saw a tiger cross the river making its way towards the town. If the people were not warned soon, the tiger would attack them. Helen swooped down to the tallest roof in town and started shouting warnings. Hearing her, the townspeople laid out food for the tiger and went indoors. The tiger came, ate and left peacefully. Helen had saved the town!

23. April Fools

It was April Fools' Day and Jessica wanted to scare her sister, Janet. She put on a scary glow-in-the-dark skeleton mask and hid behind the door. Janet was also planning a prank. She bought an ugly zombie mask to scare Jessica. Wearing it, she walked into their bedroom.

Jessica had been waiting for her sister. She jumped out from behind the door just Janet was walking in. Both the sisters stared at one another for a second. Jessica saw a zombie and Janet saw a glowing skeleton. They both screamed with fright! Their parents heard the noise and came running to see what the ruckus was about. Both Jessica and Janet pulled off their masks. Their parents had a hearty laugh at their backfired pranks.

24. The Tightrope Walker

The tightrope walker at Calamari Circus had just quit his job to become a baker. The circus needed a new tightrope walker, but they didn't know where to find one.

They held auditions and saw many candidates, but nobody impressed them. They all left the audition tent, feeling dejected.

A tree-climbing frog was passing by. It saw the empty tent with the tightrope and jumped inside. The frog stepped on the rope and started dancing as he crossed it. The frog hopped, skipped and did cartwheels on the rope with its sticky feet. The circus manager came into the tent and observed the frog. He was perfect for the job! The tree-climbing frog became the star of the circus. The people loved him!

25. Gaffy Helps Out

Cassie's father worked at the zoo. They lived on the zoo premises. Some of the tamer animals were allowed to roam near Cassie's house. One evening, Cassie's family returned from an outing and realised that they did not have the house key. As they stood there wondering what to do, Gaffy the giraffe came nearby. He nudged Cassie's shoulder gently. Cassie soon understood what Gaffy was saying. She quickly climbed onto his back and up his long neck. Gaffy stuck his head near the open window and Cassie went inside. She ran to the door and opened it for her parents.

26. The Two Ghosts

Late one night, Dr. Brown was returning home from after visiting a patient. But it was raining so heavily that the doctor could barely see anything. Suddenly, his car broke down.

It was late and there was nobody on the street.

Dr. Brown thought that he would have to spend the night in his car. Just then, he saw a light in the distance. "Oh, a house!" thought the doctor. "Maybe they will be able to offer me food and shelter for the night." When Dr. Brown knocked, an old man opened the door. He gave him food and shelter for the night.

The next morning, when Dr. Brown woke up, he saw that the house was empty. "That old man was a ghost!" he thought, rushing back to his car. The truth is that the old man had just stepped out to buy milk. When he returned, he was shocked to see the house empty. "Surely the visitor from last night was a ghost," he thought.

Both Dr. Brown and the old man told all their friends how they had seen a real ghost.

27. The Arrogant Weightlifter

The town of Mardi had a very arrogant weightlifter. He always liked to boast about his strength. All the townspeople were irritated with him. One day, the weightlifter was walking on the outskirts of the town when he saw a thin man lifting a car with

his hands! The weightlifter was shocked and scared. If this thin man came to his town, no one would respect him anymore.

"Where are you going, sir?" asked the weightlifter.

"I can't decide whether to go to Mardi or Samedi," replied the thin man. "Which do you suggest?"

The weightlifter told the man to go to Samedi. It was a close save! He became humble from then onwards.

28. The Explosive Dog

Pax the farm dog had a bad habit of eating whatever he saw. He would eat all kinds of rubbish without even thinking about it. Once, there was a small bundle of red dynamite on the farm. Pax thought it was a bunch of sausages and gobbled it up.

Soon Pax felt a strange sensation in his stomach. He opened his mouth to burp and it became a loud explosion! Everything around him shook and Pax's face became black. He kept burping explosively all day. By the end of the day, Pax was completely black with soot. He vowed to be more careful with what he ate.

29. The Special Scarf

Greg had many pairs of gloves. Every winter, he would get a few new pairs and the old ones would be ignored. One morning, when Greg opened his drawer, a pair of gloves

jumped out. "You've been ignoring all of us," they said to Greg. "But we are still good and can keep you warm." Greg simply shrugged. "Sorry, gloves," he replied. "You don't fit me anymore!"

The gloves went back to the drawer and came up with a plan. The next day, when Greg opened his drawer, all his old gloves had joined hands and fused themselves into a beautiful scarf. From that day onwards, Greg had the warmest, most colourful scarf!

99

30. The Brave Delivery Boy

Derek the delivery boy was on his way to deliver food to the Ming family. When he reached, he saw two delivery boys already at the front door.

Derek quickly realised what was going on. His boss had warned them about burglars who tapped restaurant phone calls and visited the customers' homes to rob them. Derek acted quickly. He was holding boxes of hot food in his hands. He threw them hard at the robbers' heads.

The boxes opened and the scalding sauces and gravies fell all over the robbers. They started shouting in pain.

Just then, the police arrived. The Mings had heard the commotion and called the police. They thanked Derek for saving their lives, even though he had spilled all their food!

31. Lost in Translation

Mike was visiting Tokyo and needed directions to his hotel.

But he didn't know a word of Japanese. So, he showed a passer-by the address and asked him to draw the path on his map.

The passer-by marked the path with a pen and Mike followed the directions.

But when he reached the place, he saw that he had been given directions to the zoo instead of the hotel! Mike decided to look around while he was there.

Then, he asked someone else to mark the route to the hotel on his map. This person also did not speak English, but he marked a route for Mike to follow. But this time, Mike ended up in a mall! "Well," he said. "I might as well shop while I'm here."

Mike shopped until he was tired and hungry. He asked a couple of students for directions to a nearby restaurant. They marked another route on his map and as usual, Mike followed it. But when he reached there, he saw it was not a restaurant, but his hotel! Mike may have gotten lost, but at least he got to see some of the city.

1. The Magic Lasso

Garth the cowboy had just been given a magic lasso. All he had to do was swing it in the air and the lasso would bring him whatever he wanted. Garth wanted to see if the lasso really worked. He swung it around and asked for the moon. With a loud thud, the moon landed at his feet.

The moon was angry. "Why have you brought me here?" it asked. "It's almost evening. I have to be at work soon."

"Sorry, Mr. Moon," Garth replied sheepishly. "I was just trying to see if my lasso worked." The moon rolled its eyes. "All right then. Send me back now," it said.

Garth tried telling the lasso to send the moon back, but it was useless. The lasso could only bring things, not take them back. Garth didn't know what to do. Suddenly, he had an idea. He tossed the lasso to the sky. "Mr. Sky," he called out, "Ask the lasso to bring you the moon!" The sky swung the lasso and soon, the moon zoomed back into its place. The sky dropped the lasso back into Garth's hands. "Thanks, Mr. Sky!" Garth called out, and decided to use his lasso responsibly.

101

2. Machine Gun Ellie

The paintball tournament of the Annual Forest Games was in progress. The elephants were to play against the monkeys. The elephants were worried. They were huge animals and dodging paintballs would be difficult. The monkeys, on the other hand, were small and agile.

But Ellie the elephant was not nervous. She had an idea! She told all her team-mates to put the paintballs in their trunks. When the monkeys came, the elephants used their trunks like machine guns, shooting out paintballs one after the other. They took the monkeys by surprise! Before they could even throw the paintballs, they were fully drenched in paint.

The elephants won the match, all thanks to Ellie's brilliant idea.

3. Pasta Problem

Lisa wanted to surprise her mother for her birthday. She decided to cook her some pasta. Lisa followed the cookbook's instructions and put the pasta to boil. Once it was done, the cookbook said to strain all the water out.

But Lisa could not find the strainer anywhere. She searched every shelf and cupboard, to no avail. Just when she thought her dish was going to fail, Lisa got an idea. She went to her mother's closet and found a brand new pair of stockings. She tore off the packaging and used the thin mesh stockings to strain the pasta.

When Lisa's mother came home, she was happy to see the pasta. She laughed when she heard how her daughter had ruined her stockings.

4. The Tree House

There was a tree house that travelled from tree to tree. It was special because only lonely children could see it. Kids who had no friends would wake up and suddenly find a lovely tree house in their backyard, filled with books, games and toys for them.

One morning, Shay woke up and saw the tree house sitting on a tree in her backyard. She ran to it and played all day. But the next day, the tree house disappeared. Shay went all over town, looking for the tree house. As she searched, she met three other kids doing the same. At the end of the day, they didn't find the tree house. But they all became good friends and were not lonely anymore.

5. Banjo

Banjo was a strange dog. He could climb trees and loved to swim. Banjo soon became an expert climber and swimmer. He was appointed the animal fire marshal of the area. In case a fire broke out, it was Banjo's duty to see all the animals to safety.

One unfortunate evening, a fire cracker set a dry tree on fire. Banjo ran to the spot and made sure all the animals were safe. Then, he saw a small kitten stuck on a high branch of the neighbouring tree. Banjo held his breath and climbed up the tree. He took the kitten in his jaws and climbed down.

The kitten licked Banjo to thank him.

All the animals cheered and applauded Banjo's bravery. He was a hero!

6. Daddy Long Legs

Mr. Taylor was lovingly called Daddy Long Legs because he walked on stilts that were 10 feet high. He used his stilts to do good deeds and help out his fellow villagers.

One day, the village kids asked Daddy Long Legs to find their lost kite. He agreed and took one child on each shoulder. The others trailed behind him as they went looking for the kite. They looked on top of every tree and building, but couldn't see it anywhere.

When they thought the kite was lost for good, they saw it lying in a field of corn. Daddy Long Legs reached the field quickly with his long strides. He rescued the kite and returned it to the kids.

104

7. The Banana Suit

Albie's favourite fruit was the banana. He loved it so much that he dressed up as a banana for the school's costume competition. That day, everyone was allowed to bring their pets to school. Albie's friend brought his pet monkey along. The monkey saw Albie and thought he was a big banana! It started chasing Albie. The monkey chased Albie up and down the stairs and through the library. Albie ran straight onto the stage where the costume competition was being held. The judges saw Albie being chased by a monkey and awarded him the first prize! He then changed into his regular clothes and the monkey finally left him alone.

8. The Note

When Emma got home from school, she saw that her mother was not there.
She checked the fridge to see if she had left a note for her. Emma saw that there was a note. But when she read it, she was very puzzled. All it said was "378."

Emma wondered what "378" meant. It was too short to be a phone number. It was too long to be a grocery list tally! Could it be a ransom amount? What if Mother had been kidnapped for 378/-? To the little girl, it sounded like a big amount. She was convinced that her mother was being ransomed.

Emma phoned her father at work and told him that Mother had been kidnapped. Emma's father rushed back home. Just as Emma handed him the note, Mother walked in. Imagine how confused she was when Emma and Father were so happy to see her! She explained that the number was just the house number of a new neighbour who she had gone to help move in. Everyone laughed at Emma's foolishness. But Emma was glad that her mother was fine.

9. The Time-traveller

Neville was a time-traveller. He went on dangerous missions across time to save the world from destruction. His latest mission was to help the caveman discover fire. When Neville reached the cavemen's colony, he saw that they were being terrorised by sabre-toothed tigers. That's why they had no time to make fire.

Neville made a pile of dry twigs and lit it on fire with his matches. The sabre-toothed tigers got one look at the fire and ran away. Neville showed the cavemen how to rub dry twigs to create fire. The cavemen thought Neville was the Fire God. They tried to tie him up and worship him. Thankfully, Neville had his time-travelling watch. With a push of a button, he vanished from there and went back to the present.

10. Hungry Aliens

For his next mission, Neville had to go to the future and save the world from a group of aliens. These aliens were hungry for trees. They were planning to attack Earth and eat all of its green trees. Neville had a plan. He met the alien leader with a huge cactus plant and some poison ivy. He offered the plants as a peace offering. The aliens ate the cactus plant and the poison ivy. In no time, they got the worst stomach ache they ever had.

"The trees of Earth are bad," they cried and abandoned their plan. Once again, Neville had saved the Earth!

11. The Battle of the Strawberry Flavouring

After saving the world from tree-eating aliens, Neville was asked to go to the planet of the chewing gum bunnies, which protected the entire Universe against bad breath. But someone had stolen all their strawberry flavouring and they couldn't make gum. Neville, along with an army of chewing gum bunnies, searched the entire Universe.

They found the strawberry flavouring on the planet of the ice cream cones.

Neville and the army of bunnies fought the cones with giant plastic straws.

They defeated the cones and took back the strawberry flavouring. The Universe was safe from bad breath once more.

107

12. The Ladybug's Miracle

Mrs. Bugsy the ladybug was very worried. She had lost her wedding ring and couldn't find it anywhere. She searched the patches of grass and all the leaves she had walked on, but she couldn't find it. She returned home and told Mr. Bugsy about it. "Don't worry," he said. "You will surely find it tomorrow." Mrs. Bugsy slept fitfully that night. "Only a miracle can help me," she thought. The next morning, she found that every leaf and blade of grass was covered in dew. The dew drops worked like magnifying glasses. She easily spotted her wedding ring sparkling on a leaf in the distance. She ran towards it and picked it up, happy to have found her valuable ring.

13. The Flower Attack

Every day, naughty children would come to the garden and steal all the mangoes on the mango tree. But they didn't know that the flowers were paying attention to them. These flowers were trained for combat. They decided to help the mango tree.

As soon as the naughty kids came nearby, the flowers launched a thorn attack. "Ow! Ow!" yelled the kids, as the small thorns pricked their legs. Then, the flowers launched a smell attack. The kids wrinkled their noses at the rotten smell.

It was horrible!

The naughty kids ran away as fast as they could. They decided not to go anywhere near the strange garden ever again.

The flowers were happy that they had saved the mango tree.

14. The Raindrop and the Pebble

A little drop of rain fell on a pebble. They became good friends. But sadly, the raindrop got washed away with the rain and flowed into a river. The raindrop was sad to leave the pebble, but there was nothing that she could do. She flowed from the river into the sea and there, she joined a wave. As soon as the wave reached the beach, she saw a familiar pebble on the shore. The pebble recognised her, too.

"Hi friend," said the pebble. "When you got washed away, I followed you into the river. But a bird picked me up and dropped me on the beach."

The raindrop and pebble were happy. Nature had separated them, but it had also brought them back together!

15. The Handkerchief

Joan had gone for a walk up a hill. There was a pretty little stream flowing alongside her. Joan decided to dip her feet in the water. But the rocks in the stream were slippery and she fell down. Joan could not get up. She had twisted her ankle and it was hurting her. Joan knew that she needed to get back home. She thought of a plan. Sitting down on the bank, she took her handkerchief from her pocket. She also had a pen with her. "Help. I'm sitting upstream and I'm hurt," she wrote on the handkerchief. Joan put the hanky in the stream and hoped that someone would find it.

A group of people were hiking along the same path. They spotted the hanky in the stream and fished it out. On reading the message, they hurried upstream and found Joan. They called Joan's parents and took her to the doctor. Joan's foot was put in a cast. It would heal in a few days. Everyone congratulated Joan for her quick thinking.

109

16. The Coins

One day, a boy stuck a wad of chewing gum on the table. There were two coins nearby. They both got stuck to each other with the chewing gum. The coins tried to separate themselves, but they could not. The chewing gum was too sticky.

The coins went to the kitchen and asked if anyone could help them. The oil tried,

as did the jam. But neither was successful. The coins just got oily and stickier. Finally, the butter came to help. The chewing gum was no match for the butter. The coins got unstuck immediately. They washed themselves and went their separate ways. The butter was glad to have helped the coins.

17. The Best Pizza

Joe's favourite food in the whole world was pizza. He could eat pizza all day, every day. Joe wanted to taste the best pizza in the world and decided to travel around the world to find the perfect pizza.

Joe stopped at every town and in every city that sold pizzas. Some pizzas had great toppings, others had a crunchy crust. But none of them were perfect in every way.

Joe returned home without fulfilling his dream. But he had hand-picked the best ingredients from around the world. Joe played around with these ingredients until he had made the best pizza.

Joe opened his own pizza shop and his pizzas became world-famous.

18. The Washing Machine

The washing machine was tired of washing clothes every day. It was jealous of the other appliances. The refrigerator only had to keep things cold and the microwave only had to heat things. If only the washing machine's job was so easy!

The washing machine decided that from the next day, it would also start working like the fridge.

Soon everyone would see that a washing machine was better as a fridge and it wouldn't have to wash clothes anymore. So the washing machine took all the clothes and froze them. It repeated the same thing on the next day. But soon, the washing machine got bored. It missed all the splashing around. It went back to being a washing machine and realised that it had the best job.

111

19. The Eclipse

The tribal people of Coho Island liked to roast and eat the poor zebras. On one full-moon night, the people had managed to catch two zebras. They were about to roast them, when one zebra spoke up. "If you kill us," it said, "your Moon God will be very angry." The people just laughed. "If you don't believe me," the zebra continued, "for the next few seconds, the moon will go dark to show how angry it is."

The very next moment, true to the zebra's words, the moon became very dark! The tribal people were dumbstruck. They bowed to the zebras and apologised to them. What the tribal people didn't know was that the moon blacking out was just a lunar eclipse. The smart zebras were saved!

20. The Snowman's Nose

When Ava woke up one winter morning, she looked outside and saw everything covered with snow. She bounded outside to play in the snow. Ava decided to make a big, fat snowman on her front yard. She gave him a scarf, a hat, two buttons for eyes and a carrot for a nose.

At night, the snowman came to life. "Oh no," said the snowman. "I have a carrot nose! I'm allergic to carrots." So the snowman set out to look for another nose. He found a twig, but it was too long. He found a turnip, but it was too squat. The next morning, Ava was surprised that her snowman had moved. He was now in the backyard near the turnips.

The following night, the snowman went nose-searching again. But again, he couldn't find anything suitable. Ava had been watching him from her window. She wanted to see why he was roaming at night. When she realised his problem, she went outside and gave him a nice radish for a nose.

112

21. The Can of Soup

While shopping at the supermarket, a man had taken a can of soup from its shelf and put it with the toothpastes. The can of soup was scared and lonely.

When night came, it decided to find the soup shelf all by itself. It climbed down from the toothpaste shelf and hopped into a trolley. It wheeled past the soaps and the tall

shelves packed with big bags of chips. Then, it came to the aisle with the coffee, tea and juice boxes.

The can of soup had no idea where it was. It could not see clearly in the dark. Just when it was about to give up, the soup can heard someone call its name. Turning around, it saw that the shelf of soup cans was right behind! It took its place on the shelf and slept peacefully all night.

22. Burly's Adventure

Burly the little monster could not sleep alone during the day. Humans came out in the day and Burly was afraid of them. "Humans aren't so bad," Burly's mother told him. But Burly was still scared. He thought humans would hurt him.

One evening, Burly was just waking up when he heard a loud thump. Peeking out the window, he saw that a little boy had fallen from a tree. Nobody was there to help him. Even though Burly was scared, he went outside and helped the boy.

At first, the boy thought Burly would hurt him. But then he saw that Burly was equally afraid of him! Burly and the boy became best friends and they went on many adventures together.

23. The Cuckoo Clock

Cookie the cuckoo wasn't happy with just singing in the forest. She wanted to do something great with her life. "I must go to the city," thought Cookie. "I can become famous there." So she packed her bags and flew off in search of a good job.

She applied at a magician's office, but he already had a parrot. The zoo turned her down as well. Finally, she saw an advertisement in the paper. It read: "WANTED: Official Cuckoo for the cuckoo clock in Caraway Mansion. Must sing well."

When Cookie gave her audition, the owners were very impressed. They hired Cookie right away. Cookie's cuckoo clock became the most famous and melodious cuckoo clock in the country.

24. The Orange Waterfall

Michelle lived next to a beautiful waterfall that spouted from a mountain. It was a strange waterfall because no one knew exactly where it began. One day, when she was playing outside, Michelle saw the waterfall turn bright orange. Soon, news of the waterfall spread all over the village. That night, Michelle heard about the orange waterfall on the radio, too! Nobody could figure it out. Finally, a group of scientists came forward and explained the mystery. They had been following a river that suddenly went inside a cave and disappeared. They wanted to see where it came out. So they poured buckets and buckets of orange dye into the river, hoping that somebody would report the strange sight. That's how the scientists and Michelle got their answers!

25. The Watermelon-throwing Competition

Two countries shared a large watermelon patch on their border and would keep fighting for the watermelons. To end the fighting once and for all, they decided to have a watermelon-throwing competition. The country that managed to throw the farthest would win the melon patch.

The first country came with a huge canon. The other came with a giant catapult. But when they threw their watermelons, both melons landed on a trampoline and bounced straight back to them! Everyone got drenched in watermelon juice. The countries decided to call off the competition and share the watermelons instead.

26. The Weasel and the Witch

The good witch was in big trouble. She had lost her magic wand in the forest! She began retracing her steps and found her wand in the hands of a weasel. The weasel had been waiting for the good witch. He ran towards her and pushed her into a cage.

"See how helpless you have become," he said with a laugh. "I am the strongest now!"

"You may have my wand," said the witch. "But you do not have my talent! If you were stuck in this cage in my place, you would never be able to escape!"

The weasel was stupid. He stepped into the cage proudly to prove the witch wrong. Just then, the witch said, "Let me show you how to use the wand properly." The weasel gave her the wand and the witch freed herself. Now the foolish weasel was trapped in the cage! The good witch laughed at him and went on her way.

27. A New Song for the Village

The entire village was sad. No one smiled or laughed anymore. This was because they had lost the football championship that had been held the previous week.

Roger was tired of all the sadness. He went to the wise woman of the forest and asked her for a solution. The wise woman gave him a CD and told him to play it in

the village. Roger went to the local radio station and asked them to play the CD. Soon, the wise woman's CD was playing on loudspeakers all over the village. It was no ordinary CD. It contained magical music that made the people dance. Everyone started enjoying themselves. Even though they lost the football championship, they did win the dance championship!

116

28. The Pink Monkey

Midas the monkey loved cutting and styling hair. He decided to start his own beauty salon in the forest. He promised all the animals that he would make them look like movie stars. Everyone was very excited.

On the first day, all the animals came to get their hair styled. The beauty salon was overfull. With so many animals asking for so many different styles, Midas got confused.

He ended up cutting off the lion's mane! When the lion saw his ruined mane, he roared loudly and chased Midas throughout the jungle.

When the lion finally caught Midas, he dipped Midas in the bright pink hair dye. For the next two weeks, the jungle had a bright pink monkey!

29. The Special Catch

Patty and her friends were at a cricket match. It was the final match of the tournament. Patty had worn her favourite team's jersey colours and had carried many posters. She was excited! It was a nail-biting match. On the last ball, Patty's favourite batsman was at the crease. He swung his bat so hard that the ball flew straight into the stands. Patty stood right on her tiptoes and caught it! All the cameras turned towards her and the crowd cheered. Her team had won! The batsman sprinted up to the stands. He took the ball and autographed it for her. The next day, Patty's photograph was in all the newspapers. She had become a little celebrity! It was the best match she had ever been to.

117

30. The Pie-eaters

The band of professional pie-eaters was walking to their next competition, when they passed a town facing a strange problem. All of the town's flour had fallen into the pond and become a giant lump of dough. The pie-eaters offered to help. They told the villagers to stretch the dough into a thin sheet, so that it would get cooked in the sun. By the end of the next day, the sun had cooked the dough. The pie-eaters then asked the people of the town to bring all the jam they had along with cutlery. The pie-eaters spread the jam on the dough and began eating it. They ate all night long and by morning the giant pie was gone. The townspeople rejoiced and thanked the pie-eaters with more pie.

1. The Mystery of the Strange Symbols

For the past few days, the Lawson family had been seeing strange signs and symbols on their potato fields. The crop would be cut into funny shapes. They had no idea who was doing it or why.

They all decided to stay awake and see.

At midnight, a spaceship landed on the field. A squad of three-eyed aliens climbed out and started cutting into the crops.

The Lawsons were shocked! Finally, Mr. Lawson gathered his courage and stepped outside. "Stop!" he shouted. "What are you up to?"

The aliens seemed peaceful. "Greetings, Earthlings," said the leader. "We are looking for potato chips because this is a potato field. We love potato chips. But we cannot find them anywhere. We have been searching here every night."

The Lawsons all burst into laughter. Mr. Lawson gave them directions to the nearest supermarket. The aliens thanked them and went away.

2. The Secret Room

Dean's parents had an interesting job. They would travel all over the world restoring old castles. The latest castle to be restored was in Romania and Dean got to go with them. As they worked, they let Dean explore freely.

He went behind the castle and saw a huge garden full of trees and little marble statues. A painter was white-washing the fence around the garden. That gave Dean an idea. He stole some of the painter's white paint and poured it all over himself. Then, he waited for his parents.

When he saw them looking for him, he posed as one of the marble statues. They got the fright of their lives!

3. The Island

119

Larissa lived near the sea. There were many small, deserted islands nearby. One day, Larissa took her jetski to the sea. She decided to visit one of the small islands. When she was done exploring, she went back to her jetski. But it just wouldn't start!

Larissa was scared. She didn't have a phone or even matchsticks to start a fire signal. She started pacing around, trying to think of a plan. As she was pacing, she noticed lots of wild beetroots growing on the island. That gave her an idea. Larissa collected some beets and began to stomp on them. This released their dark colour, which flowed into the sea. All the water near the island turned a dark pink. A rescue boat saw the colour and came for Larissa.

4. Ice Fishing

Stan was sad. A few days ago, he had dropped his favourite toy truck into the pond. Every day, he would peek inside to see if he could spot it under the water. But he could not. What's more, it had snowed very heavily the previous night. The pond had frozen over! There was no way that Stan was going to find his truck.

Stan's father saw him upset and offered to take him ice fishing. They wore their warm, furry coats and went to the pond. As his father was cutting through the ice, Stan gasped. He could see his toy truck at the bottom of the pond! Stan took his fishing rod and lowered it into the pond carefully. His hooked latched onto the truck and began to reel it in.

When the line reached up, attached to the end was Stan's beloved toy! It was cold and wet, but still in one piece. Stan and his father caught some big fish that day. But the best catch for Stan was his toy truck.

5. The Diary

Jerry's school was more than a century old. It was full of winding staircases, hidden corridors and secret doors. Jerry loved to spend time at the library. It was full of old, interesting books. One day, while browsing the shelves, Jerry chanced upon a handwritten diary wedged between two books. He started leafing through it.

The diary was full of maps and directions to navigate secret passages in the school. Jerry went through a secret passage that began at the library and he came out in the gym! Jerry told his friends about the secret passages and they found one that led from their rooms to the kitchen. For the rest of the year, food kept disappearing from the kitchen and no one could figure out how!

121

6. The Great Beard

There was once a man called Mr. Greatbeard. He had the thickest, longest and silkiest beard in the entire world. He was a nice man and was always ready to help everyone. One day, the townspeople came running to him.

The dam had broken and if they didn't do something soon, the entire town would get washed away.

Mr. Greatbeard told them to collect all the logs they could find and place them near the river bank. He then tied all the logs together with his beard to create a big wall. The wall of wood held the river back for a long time. In that time, the townspeople fixed the dam.

Mr. Greatbeard saved the entire town with his great beard.

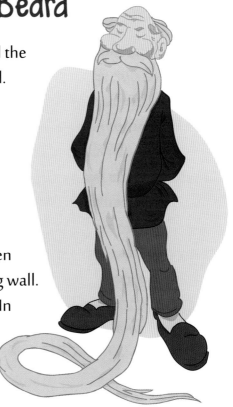

7. Jojo the Clown

Jojo was one of the finest clowns in the world. When he performed, children would laugh till their stomachs began to hurt. However, for the last few shows, none of the

children came to watch him. Jojo waited for a week, but still no children came. This made him very upset. Jojo loved children and he thought they loved him, too. The sad clown packed his things and decided to leave the circus. He went to the forest and found a cave to live in.

One day, Jojo heard the sound of children's voices. They were calling his name! Jojo scrambled out and saw all his friends. They explained that they couldn't come to see him because they had exams. But now that their exams were over, they had come to take Jojo back to the circus.

Jojo was relieved that the children still loved him.

122

8. The Ant Army

The army of ants was on a mission. There was a birthday party for their Queen and they had to get her some cake. After looking around, one ant spotted a piece of pink cake in a picnic basket across a stream. They had to find a way to get across the water. The ants began to look around for something they could use

as a bridge. They found a piece of thread, but the moment it touched the water, it lost its stiffness and sunk to the bottom. Then, they found a piece of plastic that was strong enough. They crossed carefully and managed to steal the piece of cake.

On their way back, they ran so fast that the plastic bridge almost toppled over. Finally, they reached their anthill safely with their beautiful pink cake. Thanks to them, the party was a huge success.

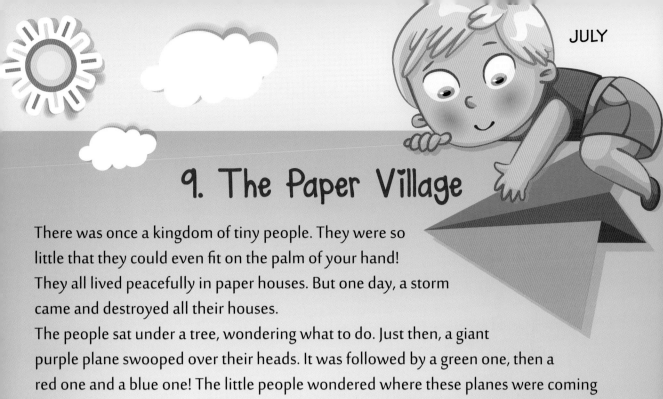

9. The Paper Village

There was once a kingdom of tiny people. They were so little that they could even fit on the palm of your hand! They all lived peacefully in paper houses. But one day, a storm came and destroyed all their houses.

The people sat under a tree, wondering what to do. Just then, a giant purple plane swooped over their heads. It was followed by a green one, then a red one and a blue one! The little people wondered where these planes were coming from. They craned their necks and saw a boy making paper planes by himself.

"If he is so good at paper-folding," said one tiny person, "maybe he could make us new houses!" So, they went up to the boy and asked for his help.

The boy was thrilled at the prospect of building an entire town. He built them a town made of thick, colourful paper. He also used strips of wood and tiny nuts and bolts to make the houses strong and sturdy. The little people named their new town after him for his kindness.

10. The Crumb Trail

Jill loved reading detective stories. Soon, she started seeing mysteries everywhere she looked! Once when Jill was walking to school, she noticed that there was a trail of breadcrumbs coming from all her neighbours' front doors.

Jill was very intrigued. Was some animal stealing bread from everyone's homes? Jill made up her mind to solve the mystery and catch the culprit.

The next day, Jill woke up early and kept a watch at the window.

Soon, she cracked the mystery.

The baker who came to deliver bread every morning had a hole in his basket. The crumbs of bread fell out, creating a neat trail. "Oh!" said Jill. "Why didn't I think of that before?" But she felt proud of herself for solving the mystery.

11. The Ball of Yarn

Old Mrs. Wan had lost her ball of yarn. Mrs. Wan asked Carol, who lived next door, to help her find it. Carol took her dog Bongo and set out looking for the wool. Bongo was following the scent of the wool. Carol let Bongo lead her around trees and under cars. Bongo kept sniffing and walking while Carol followed, looking for any sign of the wool. Then Bongo came to a tree and tried climbing it. Carol was stumped. How could a ball of wool go up a tree? But when she looked up, Carol saw Mrs. Wan's cat perched on a branch, holding the ball of wool. The naughty cat had run off with the wool. Carol climbed up and brought the cat and the wool down. Mrs. Wan was delighted!

12. The Switch

Leslie had moved into a new house. It had many rooms and she was having a good time exploring. She wandered up and down the stairs, opening every door and flicking each switch on and off just to see what it did.

In Leslie's room, there were four switches: one for the fan, one for the light, one for a plug and a fourth one that seemed to do nothing. Leslie flicked the fourth switch on and off a few times. Each time she did so, she heard a small creak coming from somewhere in the room. Leslie looked carefully and saw that the switch opened a small secret compartment in the wall behind the book shelf. Leslie decided that from then on, she would hide her most precious things there.

125

13. The Crystal Ball

Ella was studying to be a witch. One of her subjects was crystal-gazing. Ella wasn't very good at it. Most of her predictions were horribly wrong. But Ella kept practising at least twice a day. One day, when Ella gazed into the crystal ball, she was horrified to see a house go up in flames. She couldn't recognise the house and had no way of warning the owners. She immediately told her mother what she had seen. Her mother comforted her and told her to relax. At night, the entire family sat down to watch a movie on television. Ella could not enjoy it because she kept thinking about the fire. Suddenly, in the middle of a scene, Ella gasped. It was the scene she had seen in her crystal ball! Ella sighed with relief that nobody's house was actually burning down.

14. Conan's Secret

Conan was a teenage ogre. Like all ogres, he was green and huge. But on full moon nights, he changed into a thin, handsome dancer who would dance all night. It was not acceptable in the ogre community to be a ballet dancer. So, Conan would go far away and dance all night. On one such night, as Conan was dancing, he saw an ogre looking at him from behind a tree.

Conan got scared and was about to run away. "Wait!" shouted the ogre. "I'm a friend!"

When Conan heard the ogre's story, he was shocked! This ogre was actually a ballet dancer and had been cursed to become an ogre every full moon night.

Conan and the ogre became best friends!

15. Under the Mountain

Kyle was trekking up a cliff one day when he fell into a crevice. The opening of the crevice was covered with grass and Kyle had not noticed it. Thankfully, he didn't hurt himself. When Kyle got up, he saw that he was inside a dark cave.

There was no way for him to climb back out. Kyle was scared. He decided to look for an escape route. He walked deeper into the cave and saw it had a natural tunnel. He could hear the sound of waves in the distance. Kyle decided to walk down the tunnel. When he reached the end, he saw that the tunnel opened onto the beach.

Kyle was glad that he was safe and also that he had escaped before dark.

16. The Shooting Star

The shooting star had an important job. As it whizzed across the sky, it had to listen to all the wishes and keep track of the wishers. Then, he would grant the wishes one-by-one. But that night, there was a problem.

The shooting star had heard a tiny voice from a remote village asking for sweets. But it had not gotten a good look at the person's face. How would it know whom to give the sweets to? Then, the shooting star had a brilliant idea.

The star made it rain sweets all over the little village. Everyone came running out of their homes to collect the sweets. The star never found out who had asked for the sweets, but it had still granted the wish.

127

17. Hannah and the Bull

Hannah wore her bright red dress and went out to play in her backyard. Her neighbours were farmers with all kinds of animals in their farm. Hannah was playing right next to the bull pen. It had a sturdy wooden fence that kept the bulls in. But Hannah noticed that one of the bulls was looking at her red dress with an angry expression. Bulls did not like red! The bull looked like he was going to ram his way through the gate and attack her. Hannah went running back home! She changed into another dress. When the bull saw her again, he didn't snort. Hannah made sure she never wore red near him again.

18. Juan and the Blizzard

Juan was travelling to his friend's house. To go there, he had to trek through the cold mountains. In the middle of his journey, he was caught in a frightful snow storm. It was so sudden and severe that Juan had to seek shelter, or he would freeze. It was hard to walk in the windy, biting cold. Juan soon got tired and slumped against a big fir tree. As he sat there, he saw a huge ball of snow walking towards him. Juan rubbed his eyes and took another look. It was not a snowball, but the legendary Yeti! Before Juan could do anything, the yeti smiled at him and invited him to his cave. Juan did not want to remain in the cold. He silently followed the yeti through the snow. Once they reached his cave, the yeti made Juan sit in front of the fire. He gave him food and shelter for the night.

Juan woke up the next morning and saw that the storm had subsided. But the yeti had gone. Juan went on his way and reached his friend's house. He never saw the yeti again, but was always thankful for this help.

19. The Lost Ring

Ruth's mother could not find her ring. She looked everywhere, but it was nowhere to be seen. Ruth helped her mother look, but even she couldn't find it. Ruth sat her mother down and asked her to list all the things she had done since morning. Her mother told her how she cleaned the house, cooked lunch and read a magazine.

Ruth thought for a while and then walked into the kitchen. She took the loaf of bread her mother had baked that morning and neatly sliced it.

As she had guessed, her mother's ring was in the loaf. It had slipped out as she was kneading the dough and had been baked with the bread.

129

20. The Wishing Well

Every wishing well has a fairy that sits at the bottom and grants people's wishes. One such fairy was sleeping on the job. When she woke up, she saw that a few coins and wishes had been tossed into the well.

But since the fairy hadn't seen who tossed them in, she was confused as to who had asked for what wish. Having no choice, the fairy decided to grant the wishes at random. So Mr. Clark, who had asked for a car, got a pearl necklace. His car went to little Alison, who couldn't even drive yet. And Mrs. Tweed got a toy kitchen set. The three wishers were very confused. They went back to the wishing well and the fairy fixed her mistake. All three wishers went home happy.

21. The Parade

It was a big day for the school marching band. They had been invited to perform at the city parade. It was going to be aired live on television. Susie played the trombone in the band. She had practised a lot and was confident that day. But when she began playing, everyone was surprised! Instead of making a brassy sound, Susie's trombone produced a low, deep rumble. Susie had no option but to keep playing until they finished their set. She was very sad. When they finished, Susie checked her trombone and found a frog sitting inside! Susie's band mates found the incident very funny. In fact, everyone did! Susie was even interviewed by reporters. That's how she learnt that even accidents can have happy endings.

22. The Bus Ride

Nelly had a bad habit of falling asleep everywhere. One day, while returning home from school, Nelly fell asleep in the bus. When she woke up, she was all alone. The bus was parked in a field. Not a single person was in sight. Nelly stepped off the bus and called out. Nobody answered. She decided to go back and wait inside. But the door was locked! Nelly was scared now. It was late and very dark in the field. Suddenly, she felt someone shake her. Nelly screamed, jerking away. To her surprise, she saw that she was back on the bus! Her friends were shaking her awake. Nelly had just had a nightmare and there was nothing to worry about.

23. A Special Tree

Melissa's brother was very ill. They had been to all the doctors in the nearby villages, but none of them could cure him. As a last resort, Melissa decided to visit the old witch doctor of the village. Nobody believed in his cures anymore. But Melissa had heard that he knew recipes for different kinds of potions and salves.

The old witch doctor told Melissa that he could prepare the cure. But for that, he needed the bark of a very special tree that grew only in the Amazon rainforest. Melissa asked for a description of the tree and immediately set out to the rainforest.

The Amazon rainforest was thick with greenery. It was filled with dangerous animals. Melissa found the tree, but there was a big snake wrapped around it. When the snake was not paying attention, she ran to the tree, snapped a branch off and ran all the way back.

Using the branch that Melissa brought, the witch doctor brewed a potion. Melissa's brother drank it and was cured immediately.

24. Mindy the Doodler

Mindy loved to doodle and was very good at it. She would doodle in all her notebooks. If you opened her books, you would see all kinds of animals, fairies and even robots!

One day, Mindy was writing a test at school. Suddenly, she got a bad cramp in her elbow. Her hand hurt when she tried to write. Mindy didn't know what to do.

She prayed for some help. All her doodles heard her and they jumped out of the notebook pages.

She told them the answers to the questions and the doodles wrote them down for her.

Mindy thanked her doodles for helping her. She passed her exam with excellent scores.

25. The Pack of Cards

A pack of cards had fallen on the beach from somebody's beach bag. A crab picked it up and buried it in the sand. It lay there for many days. Soon, the pack of cards got bored. It wanted to escape.

Every day, the waves would hit the beach with force. Little by little, the sand around the box of cards would get dislodged. Finally, there came a day when the waves took the pack of cards along with them into the sea. The waves asked the pack where it wanted to be dropped off. The pack of cards was excited at the prospect of living underwater. So the waves left it deep in the ocean. The fish enjoyed playing cards and the pack was very happy.

26. The Cycling Race

Cathy was participating in the cycling race being held in her city. The route of the race went all around the city streets.

As Cathy was riding past a market, she saw a man standing with a broken-down car. Cathy rode out of her way to help him out and get him a mechanic.

By the time she joined the race again, Cathy knew she would not win. Sure enough, when she reached the finish line, the winners were already declared. But to her surprise, she saw the man she had helped standing on the stage!

The man she had helped was the chief guest. He invited Cathy on stage and told everyone about her kind nature. Cathy received a special prize. She was happy!

133

27. The Adventurous Imps

When the Queen's necklace was stolen, everyone knew that the wizard was the thief. The wizard was a greedy and wicked man. He would use magic tricks to hide his crime. The five imps decided to teach him a lesson. They bought a very long coat and buttoned it on, standing one on top of the other. They went to the wizard's house and knocked on his door. "Sir," said the topmost imp, "I have come to work for you. I thought you could use a tall person to reach the high shelves." The wizard was happy to get a free worker. That night, the imps got off each other's shoulders, took the necklace and returned it to the Queen.

28. The Ping-pong Ball's Journey

Bouncy was Leon's ping-pong ball. One day, while Leon was bouncing him, Bouncy toppled out of the window straight into the gutter! Bouncy was scared. He had never been alone before. There were strange creatures in the gutter. The rat was the first to spot Bouncy. She chased him down the whole length of the drain. Luckily, just before she was about to catch him, Bouncy disappeared into the water. "Whew!" said Bouncy, relieved at his narrow escape. But he had spoken to soon. Hoards of cockroaches started chasing him. He bobbed up and down, trying to get away. Suddenly, he saw his owner! Leon scooped Bouncy out, cleaned him up and took him back home.

134

29. Diana in Danger

Diana was running errands for her mother. She took the money and shopping list from her mother and was on her way to the grocer. Diana was leisurely skipping along and day-dreaming. Suddenly, a man grabbed her and carried her into a dark alley. Diana tried to scream, but the man had his hand over her mouth. "Give me your money," he ordered. But Diana wasn't even listening to him. She was too busy struggling. In her panic, Diana bit the man's hand hard. The man was surprised at her strength. He shrieked and pulled his hand away.

As soon as she was free, Diana ran out of the alley as fast as she could and alerted everyone around. The people soon caught the robber and took him to the police.

A police officer took the scared Diana home.

30. Faye and Lilith

Faye was a very obedient little pixie. She listened to everything her mother had to say. But she was sad because her mother would not let her play with her best friend, Lilith. Lilith lived at the pond, because she was a water pixie. "The pond is a dirty and mucky place," said Faye's mother. "And so are the water pixies." One day, Faye's father found a toy boat. "We should all go sailing," he said. Faye had never been on a boat before. She leaned over, trying to see the fish. Suddenly, Faye fell into the water with a loud splash! She didn't know how to swim. Luckily, Lilith was nearby and saved her life. Faye's mother never stopped the girls from playing again.

135

31. The Foolish Thief

Every afternoon after school, Pam would eat a bowl of fruit as a snack. One day, Pam's mother bought pomegranates. She put the pomegranate seeds in a bowl and left them on the dining table for Pam. That day, Pam came home very tired from school. She went straight to bed and did not see the pomegranates at all. They remained on the table all night. Later, a thief peeked into the window. He was searching for small, valuable things to steal. His eyes fell on the bowl of pomegranate seeds and he gasped. "What kind of people leave rubies lying on the dining table?" he wondered. He stuffed his pockets with the pomegranate seeds and left everything else untouched.

1. The Magic Bridge

There was a magic bridge in the middle of a forest that took kids on fantastic adventures. It looked like any other ordinary bridge. But when you crossed it, you would reach a whole new place.

Marley and Jean chanced upon the bridge one day. They crossed it without knowing that it was enchanted. When they reached the other side, they were shocked to find themselves in an ice cream factory. It was full of beautiful sights and smells.

There was a huge tub of churning cream and nozzles which sprayed different flavours. The factory was run by kind little rabbits in white aprons.

Marley and Jean saw the various flavours of ice cream being churned and packaged. They were allowed to taste everything they saw. They spent the whole day sampling different flavours and giving flavour suggestions to the rabbits. Soon, it was time to leave. Marley and Jean said goodbye to the rabbits and were transported back to the bridge.

They had had enough adventure for one day, but vowed to return once again.

136

2. Lunch with Centaurs

Marley and Jean couldn't wait to see where the bridge would take them next.
The next day, they crossed the bridge and were taken to a beautiful field with centaurs
galloping about. Centaurs have the torso of a human and the bottom half of a horse.
Marley and Jean walked up to them and introduced themselves. The centaurs greeted
them warmly and invited them to a
forest feast. The food was served on
a huge fallen tree trunk. The children
tucked in while the centaurs told them
stories of their battles. The centaurs
were peace-loving creatures. But they
would not stand for evil. Once the
meal was over, the children said their
goodbyes and were transported back
to the bridge.

137

3. The Kingdom of Crayons

On the third day, Marley and Jean were transported to the kingdom of Crayons.
Crayons was very beautiful. However, the people of Crayons looked sad and
gloomy. The King of Crayons greeted the children and explained that the kingdom
of Watercolours was threatening to wage a
war and take over Crayons. "Why don't
you contact the centaurs?" said Marley.
"They will surely help you fight the
evil people of Watercolours."
The King thought it was a
brilliant idea! Marley and Jean
spent a lovely day colouring with
crayons of every imaginable
shade. They went home with big
boxes of crayons as gifts.

4. The Scuba Diver

Milo was a scuba diver who used to dive underwater for pearls. One day, when he was under the sea, he got a very bad cramp in his leg. He could not swim at all. Milo sunk lower and lower, writhing in pain. Suddenly, he heard whispering voices.

"He's human," they said. "Should we help him?" Milo turned around and saw two stingrays speaking to each other. Milo signalled to them and asked for help. The stingrays were kind and they gently led Milo to the seabed. When Milo was feeling better, he thanked them and asked them if he could do anything for them. "Please bring us some popcorn," they said. Milo brought them popcorn every day and they became good friends.

5. The Merchant of Sleep

There was a sweet-seller in the kingdom who sold the most delicious sweets. However, they were laced with a sleep-inducing potion. When everyone was asleep, the sweet-seller would rob all the houses and run away.

When the sweet-seller came to Pablo's town, Pablo had a bad toothache and couldn't eat the sweets. So, he had left his share on the table. All the other villagers ate the sweets and fell into a deep sleep. The sweet-seller went to each house and began to steal their things. The sweet-seller came to Pablo's house and saw the delicious sweets on the table. Thinking that they were home-made, he gobbled them up hungrily. Soon, he was fast asleep. When he woke up, he had been tied and taken to prison. Pablo accidentally became the hero of the day!

6. How the Princess Got a Penguin

The princess and her puppy were inseparable. Every morning, the puppy would wake the princess up and follow her around all day.

One morning, when the princess woke up, the puppy was lost. She was distressed and looked frantically for her puppy. But he was nowhere to be found.

The princess stuffed her backpack with some supplies and set out to find her puppy. She searched and searched, but to no avail. Finally, she reached a mountain peak. There she saw her beloved puppy tied up to a tree.

The princess untied him and hugged him. A jealous penguin had taken him away. "You love your puppy so much," said the penguin. "I want to be your pet too." The princess felt sorry for the penguin. When she returned to the palace, she had two pets with her.

139

7. High Up

Hailey was very scared of heights. She never went on treks or climbed trees. Hailey had a pet kitten who loved running up trees. Someone had to climb up and get him down.

One day, when everyone had gone out, Hailey and her kitten were all alone at home. Hailey took her kitten and they went out to play. The naughty kitten began chasing a butterfly. It chased it right up a tree. He sat on the branch, looking very scared.

Hailey really loved her kitten. She hated to see him scared and alone. Taking a deep breath, Hailey decided to put all her fears behind and climb up. She slowly made her way up and looked down. She was so high up! That's how Hailey managed to rescue her kitten and get over her fear of heights.

8. The Haunted Mansion

There was an old mansion that stood in Debra's neighbourhood. It was long-abandoned and in complete shambles. People thought it was haunted, but Debra never believed the rumours. Recently people even started hearing wailing from inside. Debra didn't believe in ghosts. She decided to put the rumours to rest. On a full moon night, she went to explore the mansion. True to the rumours, she heard someone wailing from inside. Debra became a bit scared. Who was wailing? She crept inside the house and followed the direction of the wailing. It was very cold inside the empty stone house. When Debra flashed her light around, she saw that there was no ghost, but just an old cat lying on the floor. It had a broken paw. The cold air was entering its wound, causing it to wail in pain. Debra took the old cat home and there was no more wailing heard from the mansion. She had solved the mystery of the haunted mansion!

9. The Mix-up

One Christmas Eve, Santa had a lot of gifts to deliver. The children had been especially good that year! He gave out gifts all night and returned to the North Pole, tired. But Santa didn't realise that two gifts had been mislabelled. Sven from Norway had received the gift meant for Ram from India. Ram, in turn, had received Sven's gift. When Sven and Ram woke up, they found gifts that they hadn't asked for. Sven got Ram's building blocks and Ram got Sven's chemistry set. On realising his mistake, Santa sent Sven and Ram each other's addresses. Sven and Ram mailed each other their gifts. Not only did they get the gift they had asked for, but each of them also made a new pen pal.

141

10. The Glowing Jellyfish

Lottie had lost one of her earrings on the beach. She was very upset because the earrings were a present from her grandma. Lottie spent all afternoon looking for it, but it was getting dark. She had to go home soon. Lottie didn't know what to do. She sat down and began to cry. Suddenly, she heard a small squeak and looked up. A glowing pink jellyfish was staring at her intently. The jellyfish squeaked a few more times. In moments, the entire shore glowed bright pink. The jellyfish had called all its friends to light up the beach! Lottie found her earring in no time! She could not stop thanking the kind jellyfish.

11. The Lost Key

Samuel's grandpa had given him a big iron key to give to his grandma. But as he was walking towards her room, Samuel heard his brother call out to him. The horse was giving birth to a new foal! Samuel forgot about the key and ran to the stables. After the fun was over, he put his hand in his pocket and checked for the key. There was nothing in his pocket except for a big hole! The key had fallen somewhere in the stable. It was nearly impossible to find the key among the horses and hay in the stables. Just then, he got an idea. Samuel got a big magnet and moved it around. He found the key in no time! When he gave it to his Grandma, she couldn't help but wonder why it smelled like horses!

12. The Cloud-maker

The cloud-maker lived on top of a hill. He would carve clouds into beautiful shapes and send them floating over the sky. One day, a cloud that he had made long ago came floating back into his room. "What's the matter?" asked the cloud-maker. The cloud told him that a boy had fallen out of a hot air balloon and would get hurt if they didn't do something fast. The cloud-maker quickly made a bed-shaped cloud and sent it towards the boy. The bed caught the boy mid-flight and brought him down gently. The boy woke up on the ground without a scratch. He was glad and so was the cloud-maker. The bed-shaped cloud still wanders around, looking for people to save.

13. Bigfoot

Evan loved playing pranks on his friends. He would plan elaborate pranks and pretend to be clueless until the very end. One day, Evan and his friends saw a set of huge footprints in the park. The footprints led off into a thick clump of trees at the edge of the park.

All of Evan's friends looked at the footprints and were convinced that they belonged to the legendary Bigfoot. They started following the trail. But the prints ended at the foot of a tree. There lay a note by it. The kids picked up the note and read it. Evan had drawn a silly face and wrote "Fooled you!" on it.

Evan's friends chased him around the park for playing a prank on them. But they had enjoyed believing that Bigfoot was actually real, even if it was only for a short time.

143

14. Cheeky Goes to School

Misha had a pet chicken named Cheeky. Cheeky was small, soft and yellow. He loved Misha and missed her very much when she went to school. One day, Cheeky hid inside Misha's bag and went to school with her. When she opened her bag in class, Misha was surprised to see Cheeky looking up at her! Misha didn't know what to do. She hid Cheeky under her desk and hoped nobody would see him. Cheeky grew bored sitting inside the desk and listening to lessons. All he wanted to do was be with Misha. Soon, Cheeky fell asleep. When it was time to go home, Misha put him in her bag and sneaked him out. She was glad he hadn't peeked out during class.

15. Underwater Volleyball

The kingdom under the sea was having its annual volleyball match. The mermaids were in form and had more points than the mermen. The captain of the mermen was quite tense. He hit the ball over-zealously and sent it right out of the water!
The ball landed on the deck of a ship. The captain of the mermen's team had to get it back. He quietly crept on board the ship when no one was looking. He picked up the ball and was about to dive back into the sea when some kids spotted him.

"Look!" they screamed.

"It's a boy mermaid!" The captain of the team swam away as fast as he could. Finally, he lost sight of the kids. He quickly dove into the sea and took the ball back to the game.

16. The Special Bath

Monica was on a vacation with her parents at a forest reserve. They stayed in a small cottage on the reserve, surrounded by greenery and wild animals. One day, Monica's father told her that they were going to have a special bath. "What's so special about a bath?" Monica wondered.

Monica's father took her to a small waterfall. There were baby elephants bathing under it! Monica was awestruck!
She jumped into the pool and splashed around. The elephants were very gentle and they showered water on Monica with their trunks. One elephant let her sit on his back. It was the best bath she had ever had!

17. Looking for Praxys

The planet of Praxys was legendary. Everyone had heard of it, but no one had seen it.
The planet was supposedly covered in diamonds and had the tastiest fruits.
No one lived on it, so there was no way to establish communication with the planet.
But there were some scrolls left behind by ancient astronomers that described
its beauty. Nobody kne w if these scrolls were genuine or fake.
Matt was fascinated with the legendary planet and it was his ambition to find it.
When he was old enough to get a spaceship flying licence, he packed his bags and set
out to find Praxys. Matt circled the galaxy, but there was no sign of Praxys.
Just when he was on the verge of giving up, his spaceship got sucked into a portal.
The portal spat his spaceship into another galaxy. Matt started exploring the galaxy
and in no time, he was hovering around Praxys!
Matt landed on Praxys and saw that it was very pretty. The planet had delicious fruits
and was full of diamonds. Matt spent a few days on Praxys and went back home.
He was happy to have fulfilled his ambition.

145

18. The Mysterious Package

Sunny's mother was a police officer. One morning, after she left for work, the postman came with a package addressed to his mother. Sunny accepted it without a thought.

But as he kept the box on the table, he heard a ticking sound coming from inside. At first, Sunny didn't think much of it. But then it struck him—what if the box had a bomb in it? Maybe it was sent by a criminal trying to get revenge. Sunny called his mother and she rushed home.

As soon as she saw the box, she burst out laughing. It was only a digital alarm clock that she had ordered over the Internet. Sunny felt a little foolish, but his mother was glad that he had been cautious.

146

19. Wango and Ashley's Day Out

Wango was Ashley's pen pal from the planet of Zarr. Wango's planet was entirely underwater and Ashley lived on Earth. After months of writing to each other, they decided to meet on the planet of Laffs. Laffs was not just any ordinary planet. The entire planet was full of rides and adventures.

Wango and Ashley sat on a roller coaster that went under a river, through a cave and spiralled around a mountain.

But when they were under the river, the roller coaster suddenly stopped. Wango had no problem, but Ashley was not used to breathing underwater. Wango calmed her down and taught her how to hold her breath. Soon, the roller coaster started again and took them out of the river. They enjoyed the rest of the ride.

20. One Night in the Jungle

Colin's uncle was a wildlife enthusiast. He often allowed his nephew to accompany him on expeditions. One night, they decided to spend a night in the middle of

the jungle.

They took their place on a special platform which was built on a tall tree.

It was built for the purpose of letting people observe animals. Colin made sure he slept during the day so that he would be awake at night.

The jungle was scary but also very interesting at night. The forest was filled with the sound of crickets chirping. An owl perched on their branch and began eating a mouse. Then, they saw a tiger chasing a deer in the distance.

By morning, Colin was completely exhausted.

But he was also very happy because he had got to see many animals and how they lived in the jungle.

21. The Purple Melon

Tweeny the toad went shopping for fruit. When he went home and cut open a watermelon, it was purple instead of red! Tweeny wondered how that could be. He asked his mother. "Hmm," said his mother.

"Had you used the knife for anything else before cutting the melon?" Tweeny certainly had.

"Yes," he said. "I used it to crush some blueberries."

"There's your answer!" cried Tweeny's mother happily. "Blue and red make purple. The blue juice left on your knife must have mixed with the red of the watermelon."

Since Tweeny found no other explanation, his mother was probably right. In any case, Tweeny decided to eat the watermelon. It was delicious!

22. Movie-making

Carlos had been given his father's old video camera. His father encouraged him to take videos of things that interested him.

Once when Carlos and his family went camping, he set the camera up on a tripod and was filming whatever wildlife there was around their tent. But there were only a few deer and lots of rabbits. Carlos was disappointed that there wasn't much else to film. He left the camera on the tripod and went to play.

Carlos forgot about the camera and it stayed on all day. In the evening, Carlos remembered it and ran to get it back. He saw that it was left on and fast-forwarded through the tape to see what he had captured.

To his amazement, he saw a bear walk up to the camera and sniff it! Then, he saw a herd of elephants walk by the camera. The elephants had white egrets sitting on their backs. The camera had also captured a fox running around. Carlos was mesmerised and showed his family what the camera had captured behind his back.

23. Pompom at the Party

Pompom was Anya's pet hamster. He lived in a cage in her room. Pompom loved his cage, but one day, he got bored of it. So, Pompom stood on his tiptoes and slipped out of the cage.

Once he was out, he ran to the kitchen to eat some cheese. Then, he decided to visit the hamster next door, because she was having a party. Pompom had a great time. He met many pets and made new friends. Pompom didn't want to go back, but he knew Anya would miss him. And he missed her, too.

Pompom came home and crept into his cage. When Anya woke up in the morning, she peeked into Pompom's cage and wondered where he got the party hat from.

24. Mrs. Moony's Bakery

Mrs. Moony was the best baker in town. The cakes and pies she baked were no match for any other bakery. Every birthday and special occasion had a cake made by her.

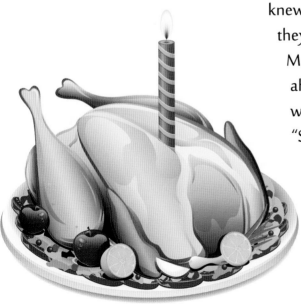

But when it was Mrs. Moony's birthday, nobody knew where to buy the cake from! After all, they could not ask her to bake her own cake. Mr. Moony had an idea. They decided to go ahead with it. On her birthday, when she walked home from work, everyone yelled, "Surprise!" But instead of a cake, there was a huge roast chicken with a candle in it! Roast chicken was Mrs. Moony's favourite food. She laughed at her substitute cake and was very thrilled that she was so loved by everyone.

25. Allen's Birthday Gift

Allen was a very good boy. Nobody had a single bad thing to say about him. Even the Sun and the Moon loved him!

On his birthday, the Sun wanted to give Allen something special. "What can I do for Allen?" wondered the Sun. "It's not as if I can give him a gift in person." The Sun thought and thought until he had an idea.

On Allen's birthday, the Sun refused to rise at his usual time. Instead, he climbed up in the sky one hour later.

So Allen got one extra hour of sleep before going to school. He was very happy and thanked the Sun after he woke up. It was the best birthday gift he could have asked for.

26. The Bully and the Bees

Bosco was a big bully. As a prank, he decided to smear honey on all the seats in class. When his classmates sat on them, ants would bite them all day. Bosco found that very funny. Everything went according to the plan and the ants began climbing on all the children. Bosco laughed at everyone. A bee was passing by the class window and saw what was going on. She decided to teach Bosco a lesson.

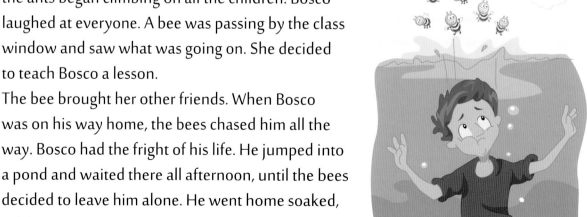

The bee brought her other friends. When Bosco was on his way home, the bees chased him all the way. Bosco had the fright of his life. He jumped into a pond and waited there all afternoon, until the bees decided to leave him alone. He went home soaked, cold and in tears. Bosco decided never to bully his classmates again.

27. The Haunted Lake

There was a small lake near Megan's home. Of late, she had heard rumours that the lake was haunted. People had seen a monster with bright red eyes inside it. Megan wanted to investigate the matter. One night, she made her way to the lake with a flashlight. She flashed her light around but saw nothing. Megan was about to leave when she saw a green head with bright red eyes emerging from the lake. She ran away quickly from the spot.

The next morning, Megan was feeling much braver. She returned to the spot and looked for the monster. When she saw it, she burst into laughter. It was just an old Halloween costume that bobbed up every time the fish disturbed it.

151

28. The Coconut Tree

A tall coconut tree stood in the town square. It housed a notorious ghost who would drop coconuts on anyone who passed underneath. Most people in the town had a nasty bump on their head thanks to him. They decided to teach the ghost a lesson.

One day, the ghost was sitting with a coconut in his hand, waiting for some unsuspecting victim. Suddenly, he felt something wet on his head. He looked up and saw a bird over his head. All day, the birds followed him around and dropped their droppings on his head.

The ghost got very angry and started yelling at the birds. "Unless you stop worrying the villagers," chirped the birds, "we will keep tormenting you." The ghost saw their point and stopped tormenting the villagers.

29. The Polka-dotted Umbrella

The polka-dotted umbrella was old. Nobody used it anymore and it felt very unwanted. One night, it ran away from home. On the way, it saw a little toad getting

wet in the rain. The umbrella stood above him, giving him shelter. After the rain had stopped, the toad thanked the umbrella. "I wish I had an umbrella," said the toad. "My family always gets wet in the rain!" The umbrella smiled. "Why don't I come with you?" it asked. "I will keep you all safe and dry!" So the umbrella went with the toad. It protected the toad family not just from rain, but also from the sun. It never felt unwanted again!

152

30. The Birthday Party

Hoho the clown was in a big hurry. He was late for Simone's birthday party, where he had to perform for her and her friends. He was stuck in traffic and was sure he wouldn't reach on time. Hoho decided to park his car at the side of the road and walk the rest of the way. It would take too long to walk along the main road, so he took a shortcut through the city's garbage dump yard. By the time Hoho reached the other side, he was covered in dirt!

Hoho jogged to Simone's house, happy that he was on time. But when he reached her house, he saw that there were no decorations or party guests. Hoho was puzzled. Simone's mother saw Hoho and burst into laughter. "Silly Hoho," she said. "You've come one day before the party!"

31. Dana's New Friend

Dana had just moved to a new school and was having trouble making friends. She was a shy girl and didn't speak to anyone. She would just go to school, sit alone in the classroom and then go home.

As Dana sat at her desk one morning, she saw a note on it with a smiley face. Dana added another smiley face and wrote "Hello!" on the paper. She left it on her desk where she had found it. For the next few days, Dana kept finding notes at her desk. She would always write replies and leave them in the same place. Dana was looking forward to meeting the writer of the notes. One day, she received a note asking her to come 10 minutes early the next morning.

When Dana went early as decided, she saw her whole class waiting for her! The entire class had been leaving the notes for her so that she would make friends with them. From that day onwards, Dana never sat alone in class.

1. The Enchanted Board Game

Chris had an enchanted board game called Werewolves and Blizzards. The aim of the game was to battle werewolves and brave through blizzards to reach the golden castle and claim it. Why was it enchanted, you ask? The enchanted part was that when you played it, you actually entered the world of the Werewolves and Blizzards!

Once when Chris and his friend Bruce were playing the game, they came across a giant squid. The squid screeched and waved its tentacles, but Chris and Bruce were not scared at all! Instead, they were confused. "The game is not supposed to have a squid in it," said Chris. "You must be some kind of mistake."

Hearing these words, the squid got very offended. To the surprise of the boys, it began to cry! Chris felt bad for hurting the poor squid's feelings. He apologised to the squid and tried to comfort it. "Don't worry, squid," he said. "You can be a part of our team!"

Since that day, Chris and Bruce never lost the game, because the squid was very strong. It braved through every blizzard and beat up all the werewolves.

154

2. The Volcano

The town of Magma was located at the foot of a volcano. The volcano had been dormant for a very long time and had not bothered the people of Magma. A boy named Mario lived there with his pet eagle. Every day, the eagle would fly around and come back to Mario by evening. One day, the eagle flew back and looked very

agitated. He tugged Mario's shirt. Mario followed his eagle to see what the matter was. The eagle flew towards the volcano crater. Mario realised the volcano was going to erupt. He ran and alerted everyone. No one was hurt thanks to Mario and his pet.

3. Ruby's Worst Nightmare

There was once a girl named Ruby who loved to sing. She had a lovely voice and knew most of the popular songs. She had promised to sing a very special song for her best friend's birthday. But on the morning of the birthday party, she woke up and found that her voice had gone. Ruby got very worried. She tried gargling, drinking warm water and taking tonics, but nothing seemed to help. She couldn't even scream. To make matters worse, her mother started shaking her insistently. She got such a start! Ruby flew awake and saw that it had just been a very bad dream. Her mother was only shaking her awake. She sang beautifully that evening.

4. The Singing Donkey

There was once a donkey who would not stop singing. Unfortunately, he was a very bad singer! One day, the village was attacked by a group of goons. Everyone was very scared. They did not have weapons to fight the goons. A boy named Hank had

an idea. He ran to the donkey and told him some people had come to hear him sing. Hank gave the donkey a microphone and told him to sing as much as he liked. The village filled with the sound of the donkey braying loudly! The goons put their hands on their ears. They had never heard anything so horrid. When it became too much to bear, they ran away from the village. The village was saved because of Hank's great idea and the donkey's terrible singing.

156

5. Spaced Out

Zuko was taking a ride through the galaxy one Saturday afternoon, when he saw the people of Planet Scaredy hovering above their planet in their spaceships. He flew up to them and asked what the matter was. The Scaredians were forced to evacuate because an army of giant cockroaches had invaded their planet.

The Scaredians were known throughout the Universe for getting easily scared and they were no match for the cockroaches. Zuko flew back to Earth to get help for Scaredy. There they loaded gallons of cockroach spray into a giant spray can.

A big spaceship carried the can to Scaredy and launched an attack on the bugs. The cockroaches quickly abandoned Scaredy and went back to where they had come from.

6. The Lost City of Rann

The legend of the lost city of Rann was known to everyone in the kingdom of Ka. It had been cursed by an evil wizard to disappear. But he also said that a child with a pure heart would find it after 500 years.

Zua lived in Ka. One day, when she was walking along the banks of a river, her puppy Shek fell into it and began to drown. The river was deep and dangerous. But Zua had no choice except to dive in and rescue Shek.

When she dived in, she saw a glow in the distance. Zua took Shek to the shore and went back to explore the light.

There she saw the entire city of Rann. It had been submerged in the river. Zua was felicitated as a hero for fulfilling the prophecy.

157

7. The Magic Orchard

Jerome's family was very poor. They only had a small plot of land and a few apple trees that grew on it. The family would sell the fruits and live off that money.

On one cold winter night, an old man came knocking at their door for some food and shelter. Jerome invited him in and fed him. Jerome's mother gave him her blanket and they made sure the old man slept well. In the morning, the old man changed into a handsome warlock. He thanked the family for their generosity and blessed them. Their patch of land grew 10 times in size and their apple trees multiplied. The apple orchard yielded twice the fruit it did in the past all around the year. Jerome's family was never poor again.

8. Pip's Mistake

Pip the flying turtle was a messenger turtle. She would take messages to and fro between witches and wizards. Pip always delivered the right message to the right wizard.

One day, Myra the witch of wonders asked Pip to write her dinner invitations. She

told her to deliver the invitations to all the magic folk. Pip wrote the notes, but instead of signing them as Myra, she wrote Nyra instead. Nyra was a miserly witch who never invited guests.

On the day of the dinner, all the magic folk came to Nyra's house for dinner. Nyra was taken aback and didn't know what to do. She was forced to throw a banquet. That night, Nyra was appreciated by everyone. She felt so good, that she stopped being miserly and made lots of new friends.

9. Cornelius the Prankster

Cornelius was a naughty cat and did whatever he pleased. He liked to play pranks and worry everyone around. One afternoon, he decided to play a prank on the Pigeon family. He switched the labels on their bottles of ketchup and hot sauce.

Mrs. Pigeon was in a good mood that day. She thought she would cook for Cornelius, as he had not done anything bad lately.

She made him a hamburger with lots of cheese and ketchup. Cornelius ate it in one bite!

Immediately, his entire face turned bright red and his eyes began to water. He yelled and ran to drink some cold water. Cornelius learnt his lesson and told Mrs. Pigeon about his prank.

10. The Library Book

Marco was very forgetful. Once, he borrowed a library book and forgot all about it. When he finally remembered it, it was already two weeks past the due date.

Marco began searching high and low for the book. He looked under his bed, inside all his bags and every other place he could think of. When he couldn't find it, he opened up his piggy bank and counted his money. He had just enough to buy a new book and replace it.

Marco bought the book and hurried to the library. But when he got there, the librarian looked puzzled. She told him that his mother had already returned the book two weeks ago! Marco sheepishly went back home and vowed to be less forgetful.

159

11. The Soapy Situation

Darryl dog's loved playing in dirt. One day, when Darryl was home alone, his dog came home covered in mud. Darryl caught him and put him in the bath tub. He filled the tub with water but did not know how much soap to put in. So he emptied the whole bottle of soap into the tub.

In a few minutes, the entire bathroom was filled with lather. It even started leaking through the bathroom door. Darryl had no idea who to do. He took his dog to the kitchen sink and washed him off. Then, he began draining all the soap in the bathroom.

When Darryl's parents came home, they found a squeaky clean bathroom and an equally clean dog.

12. The Super Sled

When the family went on vacation, the toys at home came to life. All of them were in the mood to go sledding. But there was no snow! So they took a tray from the kitchen and soaped the underside. The toys then dragged the tray on top of the stairs and tested if it slid down. It did!

The toys dragged the tray back up and piled on it. The teddy bear gave it a push and jumped on at the last minute. The tray zoomed down the stairs and straight out through the cat flap, into a pool of muck.

The toys walked back home and took a long bath. Ever since then, they stopped playing dangerous games.

13. Cross Connection

Clive had been experiencing some problems with his telephone line. Of late, he was able to overhear conversations between other people. Clive was a little nosy, so he didn't really mind.

One day, when Clive answered the phone, he overheard a conversation between two men.

"We will go tomorrow morning," said one man.

"I have checked the security and made the arrangements." The other man laughed.

"We'll clean Newland Bank out!" he said.

Clive put down the receiver and immediately called up the police. The next morning, the police waited at Newland Bank. Sure enough, two men in masks came in and tried to rob the bank. The police quickly caught them and took them to prison. Everyone was very pleased with Clive.

14. The Lost Treasure of Jade City

Vicky and Thomas were exploring the abandoned ancient city of Jade. They were looking around the city temple, when they noticed a secret door behind a huge statue. They squeezed behind the statue and entered the door.

In the middle of a huge room, they saw golden egg. Guarding it was a three-headed dragon. "Now that you have entered this room," hissed the dragon, "you must tell me a good story. If I like it, I'll give you the egg. Or else I will scorch you."

Vicky thought of the funniest story she knew. She told it with gestures and sound-effects, and Thomas even acted out some parts. The dragon burst into laughter. It allowed Vicky and Thomas to take the golden egg.

15. The Zombies' New Diet

The zombies who lived in the graveyard were running out of brains to eat. They had to make do with eating cabbages. Cabbages were not as healthy for them as brains and all the zombies were falling sick.

They decided to steal brains from the school laboratory. They crept into the school at night. But instead of going to the laboratory, they ended up in the cafeteria!

One of the zombies opened the fridge and saw a huge tub of ice cream. He tasted it. It was delicious! The zombie instantly felt stronger.

He made everyone else eat the ice cream as well. They all decided it was much tastier and healthier than brains. From then on, the zombies ate only ice cream and not brains.

16. A Feast for the King

There was once a king who loved to eat. He wanted a new dish every day. After a while, his chef grew tired and left the job. A new chef was employed. On his very first day, the king asked him to make something that nobody in the world had tasted before. The chef wondered what he could possibly serve the king.

Then, he had an idea. He took a tall glass and scooped ice cream into it. He added layers of jelly, cake and cherries. Finally, he added another layer of ice cream. When the king tasted it, he liked it so much that he decided to eat that very dish every day.

From then on, the chef's life became easy. He had finally found something the king liked and didn't have to come up with ideas every day.

162

17. Smoke Signals

A group of school kids had gone trekking up a mountain. They were not being careful or following the map. They lost their way. The sun was setting and it would be dark soon. The group didn't know what to do. They thought hard and devised a plan.

They lit a fire and made smoke signals. Once it became completely dark, the smoke signals floated across the sky and were clearly visible. Soon enough, the group saw more smoke signals float up from another place. The rest of their school group had seen their smoke signals and were replying. They went in the direction of the smoke and found their way to the base camp.

18. The Salesman

Seth was very sad. A bad accident had left him without one leg and he could not play outside like the other children.

One night, Seth was lying on his bed when he heard a sharp rap on his window. He looked out and saw a salesman smiling at him. "Hello, sir!" said the salesman. "I sell magic things. I see that you are missing one leg. I have a magic skateboard that you might like!"

Seth got very excited. "I would love that!" said Seth. "But I don't have any money." The salesman agreed to sell Seth the skateboard in exchange for any toy that Seth had. Seth gave him his joke spectacles. "Thank you!" said the salesman. "I hope to enchant this toy and make another child very happy!" With those words, the salesman left.

Seth enjoyed flying around on his magic skateboard. He would often wonder where his joke spectacles were. He did not know that halfway across the world, a blind child was able to see because of them. Just like he was able to move with the skateboard!

163

19. Felix's Eyes

Felix woke up to the sound of his ringing alarm clock. He rubbed his eyes and put on his spectacles. But funnily, Felix couldn't see anything clearly.

He washed his eyes and put on his glasses once more. His vision was still blurry.

Felix got really worried. He thought he was going blind. As he was walking towards the kitchen, his sister bumped into him. Felix told her how he was seeing blurry. But even she was having the same problem!

The siblings were confused. They went to their mother and told her what was going on. Their mother asked them to take off their glasses and exchange them with each other. The kids exchanged their glasses and saw clearly once again. Felix laughed and felt silly for being worried.

20. The New King

The kingdom of Moira needed a new king. The old king and queen planned to retire and they had no children. They started holding interviews. Many candidates came and went, but the royal couple was not impressed.

Then came the Prince of Potland. The king and queen were not very convinced with his answers, but he managed to complete every task given to him. The king and queen were suspicious. They asked their detective to follow him. The detective saw that the prince made his secretary complete the tasks. The next day, the king and queen called him to the castle along with his secretary. To the surprise of all, they crowned the secretary as the new king of Moira.

21. The Kiss of True Love

There was once a very arrogant princess. The witch decided to teach her a lesson. She put a powerful curse on the princess. She cursed her so that nobody would recognise her as the princess. Only the kiss of true love would be able to break it.

The princess was thrown out of the castle. She was lonely, sad and poor. One day, she saw a little puppy lying hurt on the road. She adopted the puppy and cared for it. When the puppy got better, he licked her face. The next moment, she turned back into a princess. The puppy truly loved the princess and his kiss had saved her. The princess became a wonderful and kind ruler.

165

22. Mr. Mow and the Zombie

Mr. Mow was coming home from the market. His arms were full with bags. Suddenly, he heard someone call out to him. He turned around and saw a zombie chasing him! Mr. Mow began running as fast as his legs could carry him. But no matter how fast he ran, the zombie kept pursuing him. Finally, Mr. Mow got tired. He slumped against a wall and waited for the zombie to attack him.

The zombie caught up with him, panting heavily. "You humans keep thinking we want to attack you," he said. "But I just wanted to return your wallet. It had fallen out of your pocket." Mr. Mow felt ashamed for jumping to the conclusion that the zombie was evil. He thanked the zombie for his kindness.

23. The Purple Potion

Sophia was messing around in the kitchen when she saw a bottle full of purple juice in the fridge. She didn't know what it was, but took a sip of it anyway. It tasted horrid. Sophia washed her mouth out and went out to play with her friends.

When she walked towards them they all stared at her like there was something wrong with her. "What's the matter?" she asked. Her friends were too shocked to speak. "J-just go and look in the mirror," they said. "You will see for yourself."

Sophia ran back home and grabbed a mirror. She was shocked to see she had bright purple ears! "Oh no!" she squealed and ran to show her mother.

It turns out that the purple juice in the fridge was a special kind of dye. It was not meant to be swallowed. "Be thankful that it did not make you sick!" scolded Sophia's mother. She gave Sophia a clear liquid to drink. After some time, her ears turned back to normal. What a narrow escape!

24. Rescue Mission

Polo the polar bear had been kidnapped by poachers. His friends got together to rescue him. A group of 10 burly polar bears hid behind the turn on the road and waited for the car to pass by. They kept some extra sharp shards of ice on the road so that the tyres would puncture and the car would be forced to stop. When the car hit the turn, it stopped and the poachers stepped out. The bears ran out from behind the tree and caught them by surprise. They tied the poachers to a tree and rescued Polo.

They went home laughing and singing over their victory.

25. Linda's Horse

Linda lived on a ranch. Her father was a cowboy. The ranch was filled with all kinds of cattle, but Linda loved spending time with the horses.

One day, her father bought a new horse. This horse seemed very angry. He would not let anyone come close to him. He had to be shut in the stable and fed from afar.

Linda was upset to hear about the new horse. "He must be very unhappy," she thought.

Linda took a bag full of apples, carrots and sugar cubes to him. When the horse saw Linda, he didn't get angry. Linda started feeding him apples every day. One day, the horse came close to her and nuzzled her. That's when Linda knew he was willing to be friends.

He soon became Linda's favourite horse.

26. At the Airport

Robin was a very mischievous boy. He always did exactly what he was told not to do. Once, he was at the airport with his parents. They were standing in the queue to board their plane. Robin didn't want to stand in the long queue. When his mother

wasn't looking, he ran and stood in a shorter queue. Robin entered the flight and waited for his parents. When they did not come, he started to panic.

He told the airhostess what he had done and she explained to him that he had boarded the wrong flight. She took him back to his parents just as the plane was about to leave! After that, Robin made it a point to follow instructions properly. No more shortcuts for Robin!

27. Hijacked

There was a terrorist who wanted his demands met. He came up with an elaborate plan to hijack a plane. Once he had hostages, he could ask for whatever he wanted.

He went to the airport and boarded a small aircraft with only a few passengers. When the flight was in the air, the terrorist sprang out of his seat and pulled out his gun. "Everyone, stay in your seats!" he yelled.

To the terrorist's surprise, nobody even flinched! "Why aren't they scared?" he wondered. But the terrorist didn't know that he had chosen to hijack a plan full of police officers on their way to an annual convention. They overpowered the terrorist, confiscated his weapon and threw him into prison. It was the easiest terrorist capture ever!

28. The Special Sweets

Eva, Lily and Nicole were at the park when they saw a box of sweets lying on a park bench. They were about to throw the sweets into the dustbin, but then they saw them sparkling with magic. Taking a closer look, the girls saw that there was something written on the box. It read: "Magic Sweets. Eat one and experience the fun!"

Eva popped a blue sweet into her mouth. Almost immediately, she started floating upwards. Eva had turned into a cloud! She floated happily in the sky, enjoying the sensation of flying. Then, Eva spotted a town that was praying for rain. She floated over the town and rained all over it.

Eva could feel the magic wearing off. She floated into the park and soon turned into herself again.

29. Lily Underwater

Next, it was Lily's turn. She picked up a red sweet and chewed on it expectantly. Immediately, she found herself underwater as a beautiful dolphin. Lily swirled underwater and swam about. She jumped up, flipped in the air and splashed back in. When she raised her head to the water's surface, she spotted a lost and tired turtle floating aimlessly. Lily swam to the turtle.

She took him on her back and gave him a ride to the shore. The turtle thanked Lily and promised to return the favour one day.

After taking the turtle to his shore, the magic faded away and Lily returned to the park.

30. Nicole the Lioness

It was finally Nicole's turn to choose a sweet. There were so many to choose from! Nicole decided on the purple one. As soon as she popped it in her mouth, she was transported to a jungle. She was a fearsome lioness!

Nicole felt really powerful as she raced through the jungle and growled loudly. As she was going past the river, she saw a drowning deer.

She jumped into the water and pulled the deer out. The deer was very surprised that a lioness had saved him instead of eating him up. He thanked her for saving his life and scampered away.

Once Nicole was back in the park, she shared her story with her friends. All three girls were happy that they had been helpful during their adventures.

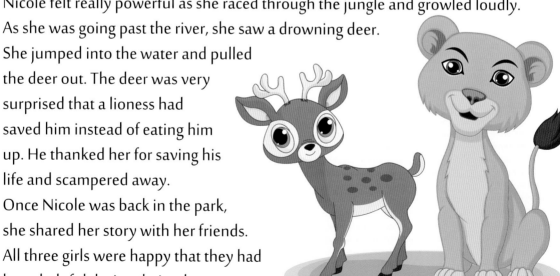

1. A Day with Dr. Cole

Martha had been given a class assignment to spend a day with someone she wanted to be like when she grew up. Martha chose her neighbour, Dr. Cole, because she wanted to grow up and become a vet just like him. Dr. Cole was flattered and took her on his rounds with him.

That day, he had to go to the Wyatt Farm and take care of their bull. The bull was very angry and was going around in circles inside his pen. No one knew what was the matter with him. After observing the bull for a while,

Dr. Cole knew it would be impossible to examine him without tranquilising him first. He took out his tranquiliser gun and shot the bull with a dart. The bull slumped down, unconscious. Martha and Dr. Cole went to have a close look at him.

They checked him carefully and saw a huge piece of glass wedged inside his hoof. Dr. Cole gently took the glass out and bandaged the bull's foot.

He prescribed an ointment for the wound. Then, they went back to the clinic. Later that day, the farmer called and said that the bull was much happier.

2. The New Fish Bowl

Pauline had a pet goldfish named Nikko, who lived in a small bowl. One day, Pauline brought home a large fish tank. She put Nikko there, thinking that he would prefer it to his small, cramped bowl.

The next morning, when she went to check on Nikko, he was not in his tank.

Pauline didn't know where to look for him.

Where could a goldfish possibly go?

What had happened was that Nikko had tried sleeping in his new tank, but he didn't like it at all. So he signalled to Jimbles the pet dog and asked him to return him to his old bowl. Finally, Pauline thought to look in the bowl and she found Nikko happily swimming around. She was happy to find him. But how he got there remained a mystery to her!

3. Grandpa's Book

Dora's grandfather loved reading. She would always find him with a book in his hands. One day, Dora returned from school to see her Grandpa looking stressed.

"Just a moment ago, I was reading my book," said Grandpa. "But now I can't find it!"

Dora looked around the entire house for the book, but even she could not find it. She asked him what he had done all day.

"All I did was eat ice cream and read," said Grandpa, shrugging his shoulders. That gave Dora a hunch. She went to the kitchen and checked again. As she had expected, she found his book inside the freezer with the tub of ice cream. Grandpa had absent-mindedly put it there when he went to have a snack. They both had a good laugh.

4. Finnegan's Fleece

Finnegan the sheep had beautiful, downy fleece. During the cold winters, he let the other animals snuggle up to him and sleep. But slowly, the seasons started to change and the weather became warmer. One day, the farmer took Finnegan outside and shaved off his beautiful fleece. Finnegan was so embarrassed! He didn't know why the farmer did something so mean. Finnegan was scared to go back to his friends. They would laugh at him. With a heavy heart, he packed his things and planned to run away and hide in the woods. Just then, a few of his friends saw him. "Nice haircut!" they all said. Nobody laughed! Finnegan was happy. Without his fleece, he felt nice and cool even in the hot summer. And when it started to get cold again, Finnegan's fleece grew back.

173

5. Feathery Tale

A group of birds were perched on their tree, chatting with each other. Suddenly, a new bird came and sat on their tree. "Hello!" said the new bird. The old group was mean-spirited. They saw that the new bird had ugly-looking feathers. They refused to talk to him and made fun of his feathers. The new bird went away, dejected.

A little while later, a huge net was thrown over the tree. All the birds were caught and their feathers were plucked out. They were bald!

That's when the new bird came back. At first, he laughed at the bald birds. But then, he plucked out a few of his own feathers and shared them with the birds. That's how they all became friends.

6. Not Just Seashells

Rose was spending the afternoon at the beach, digging for seashells. She used her digging toys to dig out the best seashells from the sand.

Rose spotted the tip of a curious-looking seashell and dug it out. It turned out not to be a seashell at all, but a very old-looking pocket watch. As she kept digging up the spot, she found more curious objects like a pearl necklace, a cuff-link and some broken china. She gave the objects to her parents, explaining where she found them.

Her parents passed them to the coast guard. Then, they went home. The next morning, Rose was surprised to see her name in the newspaper! The objects she had found belonged to a ship that had sunk many years ago.

174

7. A Slippery End

Two armed thugs stormed into the local bakery to loot it. They pointed their guns at the people present and told them to stand by the wall with their hands in the air. The cashier behind the counter was frightened, but he decided to do whatever he could to stop the robbery. The thugs told him to open the cash register and stand against the wall like all the other people. The cashier went up to the cash register and opened it. As he was walking away, he poured some icing on the floor.

The two goons made their way to the cash and slipped on the icing. Their guns flew out of their hands and the cashier ran and took them. He then tied them up and handed them over to the police. Everyone thanked the brave cashier for saving the day with his cleverness.

8. The Happy Ending

One night, Marjorie was reading a story about a prince who travelled over seven seas to rescue a princess from the clutches of an evil dragon. However, the story ended on a very sad note. Marjorie hated sad endings. She started to cry bitterly. But then, she heard a small voice whispering her name.

Marjorie looked at her book and saw that the prince on the cover was the one calling out to her! Marjorie was very surprised. "Don't cry, Marjorie," said the prince. "I don't like sad endings either. Why don't you help me make it happy?" Marjorie stepped into the book with the prince. Together, they slew the evil dragon and rescued the princess. Marjorie did get her happy ending after all!

9. The Magic Coat

Hansel was a rather ungrateful boy. He never appreciated anybody's hard work. In order to teach him a lesson, his toys enchanted his coat. Whenever he would wear it, he would become someone else for a while.

That day, when Hansel put on his coat, he turned into a gardener. He worked hard, tending to the garden. But then, he saw a puppy trying to dig up a patch of freshly-planted tulips. Hansel shooed the puppy away. Soon, it began to rain heavily. The garden became a muddy mess! Hansel realised how hard it was to be a gardener. He vowed to appreciate his gardener from then on.

10. A Firefighter's Day

When Hansel wore his coat again, he became a firefighter. Before he could react, the alarm bell rang and he was on his way to a building which had caught fire.

Hansel helped the firefighters extend the ladder and rescue the people. Everyone was evacuated except an old man who was trapped inside his bathroom.

Hansel knew he had to help him out.

He went up the ladder to the man's window. There was black smoke everywhere and the old man was coughing continuously. Hansel helped him climb outside the window and down the ladder. Soon, the old man was on the ground, safe. Hansel was proud of himself.

He realised how important and dangerous a firefighter's job was.

176

11. Bullfighting

Hansel put on his coat, wondering where he would go next. He was starting to understand how tough other people's lives were.

He found himself standing in a ring surrounded by a huge crowd cheering him on. There was a red cloth in his hands and an angry bull in front of him. It charged at Hansel in full speed. Hansel quickly realised that the bull was interested in the cloth and not him. Just as the bull was about to ram into the cloth, Hansel flicked it aside. The bull kept chasing him around until it was tired. Finally, it went back into its pen. Hansel was declared the winner. He felt deep respect for bullfighters, who had a very difficult and dangerous job.

12. The Principal's Point-of-view

Hansel had experienced being a gardener, a firefighter and a bullfighter. He had no idea in whose shoes he would be put in next. To his sheer surprise, he became the principal of his school!

Nobody liked the principal because he was meant to be very strict. Hansel thought he would give everyone a holiday, just for fun. As soon as he was about to make the announcement, a teacher walked in. She told him about how she was concerned that her students would not pass. Then, the janitor walked in. He complained about how dirty the students left the school. Hansel heard many more such complaints.

That day, Hansel realised that teachers gave them work not to worry the students, but because they cared for them.

After seeing a big change in him, Hansel's toys removed the enchantment from his coat. From then on, Hansel always appreciated people and made sure to thank them.

177

13. Puppy to the Rescue

Pax the puppy had just been adopted by a new family. He was very happy in his new home. He loved everyone, especially Grandpa. One morning, everyone left for work and school. Grandpa and Pax were the only ones at home.

When Grandpa was moving about in his wheelchair, he slipped down the stairs and fell. Pax got very worried. He scrambled outside the window and started barking very loudly. His barking caught the attention of a police car. When the policeman stepped out, Pax grabbed the leg of his trouser with his teeth and dragged him towards the door. The policeman broke the door and found Grandpa. When the family learnt about the incident, they all praised Pax. Little Pax could not stop wagging his tail!

14. Kevin's Toys

Kevin was a naughty boy who would mistreat and break his toys. So, all of his toys would hide under the sofa. Kevin's toys would keep disappearing and he would keep buying new ones. But they all ended up under the sofa. Soon, there was no more space underneath the sofa. The toys decided to move away to the second-hand shop, where some kinder children would buy them. When the toys were leaving, Kevin saw them and began chasing them. But in the garden, he slipped and hurt his knee.

Kevin went home crying and decided to be nice to his toys. His old toys never returned, but all of Kevin's new toys were treated with lots of love.

When her sister went to camp, Jasmine had to sleep alone in their bedroom. She was very scared of the dark. She kept looking at the window nervously from her bed.

Just as she was about to fall asleep, she saw an ugly green monster peeking through her window! He had smelled Jasmine's fear and come searching for her.

Jasmine froze with fright. She couldn't even scream. The ugly thing climbed in and came towards her. Jasmine knew everyone was asleep and she would have to defend herself. She threw her pillows at him. Then, she hit him with her baseball bat. She even threw her teddy bear at him! But he seemed unaffected.

Finally, Jasmine rolled up her math textbook and hit him with it. The monster shrieked.

"Anything but the math book!" he cried.

"Go away now," Jasmine said, with new courage. "If you don't, I will make you solve equations!"

The monster ran away as fast as he could. From that day onwards, Jasmine was not scared anymore. She had her math book to protect her!

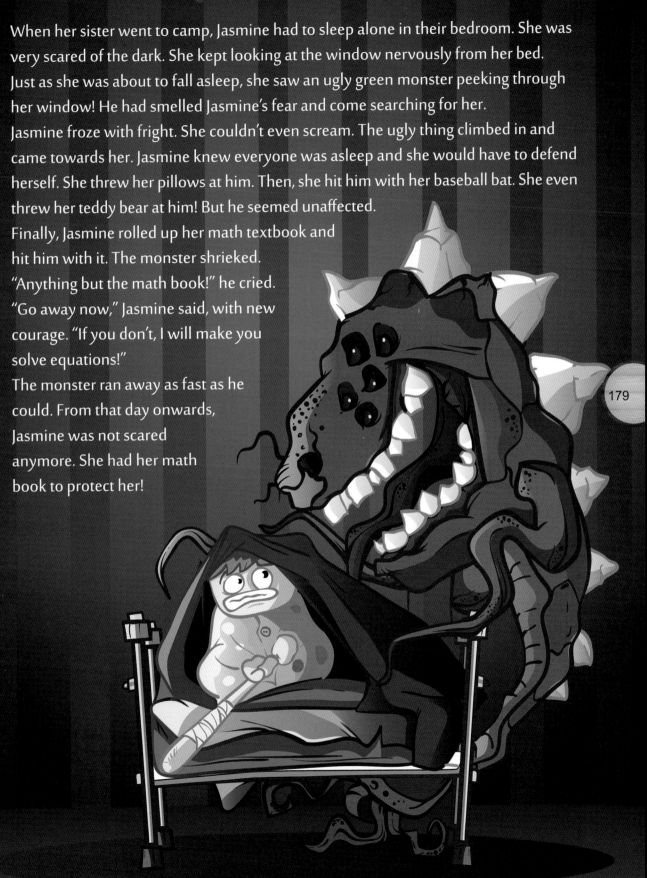

179

16. The Concert

Riley Cyprus was the newest pop singer on the block. All the kids were attending her concert. Mabel wanted to go too, but she fell ill at the last minute. When her friends came back from the concert, they couldn't stop singing Riley's songs. In fact, they

even said that Riley should be the new president of the country! Mabel was worried. All her friends had turned into mindless worshippers of Riley. Mabel searched online for a cure for brainwashing. One site suggested bathing the victims with eggs.

So Mabel threw a whole pail of eggs on her friends! Everyone was so surprised with Mabel's action that they forgot all about Riley Cyprus!

17. Wolfgirl

Wolfgirl was the superhero of the forest animals. One day, she was given a mission to investigate the strange purple fumes rising from the fox's lair. Wolfgirl stealthily made her way to the lair. There, she saw the fox mixing ingredients into a large cauldron. "Hehehe," cackled the fox. "I'll poison all the animals with this soup!" Wolfgirl had to stop the fox. She rang his doorbell. By the time the fox came to open the door, Wolfgirl jumped in through the window. She quickly took the fox's poison soup and poured it into his dinner dish. Before the fox could return, she sneaked back out. The fox drank the poisoned soup and fell sick for an entire year! That was the last time he plotted against anyone.

18. The Rain Dance

The villagers were worried. It hadn't rained for a year. The lake was running dry and the crops were suffering. Soon, they would completely run out of water. The oldest man of the village suggested that they try the ancient rain dance ritual.

All the villagers gathered on the grounds and lit a bonfire. The old man started first. Singing a strange song, he slowly began dancing around the bonfire. The other people slowly joined in, mimicking his sounds and movements. The villagers danced late into the night, but nothing happened. When they woke up the next morning, they found that it had rained all night! The villagers were very happy.

19. The Red Scarf

The sailor's red scarf had become old and frayed. He knew that it was time to buy a new one. But the sailor couldn't just throw his favourite scarf away. The scarf, too, didn't want to stay locked in the trunk.

During a storm, the ship was stranded in turbulent seas. There was no way for the sailor to contact the port for help. Then, he had an idea. He took the red scarf and tied it to the highest mast. The bright red scarf fluttered in the wind. Soon, a rescue helicopter came down and lifted the sailors off the ship. They had spotted the vessel because of the red scarf. Happy with his life, the proud scarf sank with the ship.

20. Cherry's Yummy Adventure

Cherry was a nosy cat. He loved to see what others were up to. One day, Cherry was sneaking around town as usual, peeping through everyone's windows. Suddenly, he saw a rather strange sight. His neighbour Rick had a jug that was pouring milk into his cup on its own! Rick snapped his fingers and the jug stopped pouring.

"Tea," said Rick and clapped his hands. The jug began pouring tea! Again, Rick snapped his fingers and the jugged stopped pouring. Cherry wanted this magic jug for himself. So, when Rick wasn't looking, he stole the jug.

"Cream," Cherry said. He clapped his paws together and the jug began pouring cream. But when he wanted to stop the jug, Cherry realised that he had no fingers! "STOP!" he yelled, to no avail. Cream filled his room, his house and began overflowing onto the street. Cherry ran to Rick and told him everything. Rick laughed and snapped his fingers, causing the jug to stop. Cherry was relieved. But he spent the next three days cleaning his house!

21. Running to School

One morning, Franny woke up very late. She was going to be late to school! She rushed through her morning tasks and bounded out. She didn't even stop to eat her breakfast or say goodbye to her mother.

"Franny, wait!" called out her mother.

But Franny had no time. She ran off quickly. Franny ran all the way to school, huffing and puffing. When she finally reached, the gates were closed! No other person was in sight.

Franny looked around for some explanation. Then she realised that it was a holiday!

Franny finally understood why her mother was calling her back. She wished she had waited to hear her out!

22. The Mango Thief

Gordon loved visiting his grandmother in the summer. She had many mango trees and Gordon loved eating the delicious fruit. But when he reached Grandma's house, she met him with a long face.

"I'm sorry," said Grandma. "There are no mangoes this time. A ghost has been stealing them all." Gordon found this rather odd. What sort of a ghost steals mangoes? So he decided to investigate. He poured oil on the trunk of the mango tree and hid. At around midnight, a pale white ghost appeared and started to climb the tree. But the oil had made the trunk slippery. The ghost slipped and fell, and the white sheet slid off! Gordon saw that it was only a thief pretending to be a ghost so that he could steal the mangoes.

23. Cupcake Land

Cupcake Land was the hardest place to find in all of Foodland. The road to the land of cupcakes was a closely-guarded secret. Very few, privileged people were allowed to go there. Brian made it his mission to find Cupcake Land. He asked everyone on Brownie Street, in Chocolate Pool and even on Candy Road if they knew how to get there. But nobody knew. Those who knew pretended not to. Then, Brian got an idea. He went to the wishing well in Lollipop City. Brian wished to go to Cupcake Land. To his delight, a spiral staircase rose out of the well and all the way through the clouds. Brian climbed up and found that Cupcake Land was actually built on the clouds!

184

24. The Turkish Towel

The blue Turkish towel was very loyal. It was a lovely towel that took pride in its work. It would make sure that its master was completely dry after his bath. One day, its master had a big meeting. He dried himself in a hurry and rushed off. The Turkish towel saw that its master's ears were still dripping wet. It didn't want its master to look shabby in front of others. So the little towel followed its master all the way to his office.

When the towel finally caught up with him, he was in a meeting. Despite that, the towel went in and began wiping his ears! Everyone laughed at the situation. The towel got an encouraging pat for its dedication.

25. River Brone

River Brone was a mighty river. It had a strong current that rushed past villages, towns and cities before it finally went to the sea. The Brone was too strong for humans to swim in, but many people didn't understand that. They would try to enter it anyway. The Brone would do its best to keep them safe, but it was a difficult task.

Once, when it was passing by the city, it saw a group of humans gearing up to come rafting inside it. The Brone knew that if the humans stepped in, they would injure themselves on the rocks. What could it do? It decided to take a grave step. To warn the people, it turned all its water to a bright shade of red.

Everyone who saw the Brone that day got scared and refused to go near it. The group that wanted to go rafting too had a change of heart. The Brone felt proud of itself for coming up with a unique and effective warning. It never had to worry about the people's safety again!

26. Ron's Midnight Adventure

Ron was fishing in the sea. Suddenly, he felt a strong tug on his fishing line. He reeled in the line and hauled in the biggest fish he had ever seen! To his surprise, the fish started speaking. "I am the king of this sea," said the fish. "If you let me go, I will give you a reward at midnight."

Ron was curious. He let the fish go and went to the sea at midnight. True to his word, the king fish was waiting with many other underwater creatures. All the water animals started singing and dancing for Ron. It was quite a beautiful sight! Ron danced, sang and celebrated with them until morning.

186

27. The Mask

Rory was hiking in the forest with his brother. Suddenly, they found a strange-looking mask lying in a clump of bushes. They picked it up and examined it closely.

Rory could feel a strange energy coming from it. He tried it on. Immediately, the mask got stuck to his face. He couldn't take it off, no matter how hard he tried. Rory's brother also tried pulling it off him, but he could not. Rory was afraid he would have to live the rest of his life behind a strange mask. He began to cry. Rory cried so much, the inside of the mask got wet and slippery and fell off. Rory and his brother ran away from it as fast as they could. There was no saying what would happen if they tried touching it again. Rory was relieved that he had escaped.

28. The Cruel King

Once upon a time, in a faraway land, there was a poor farmer who lived with his family. The king of the land was very cruel. He would take the farmer's fruits without paying him. One year, the farmer had a bad harvest. He would not have enough fruits for the king.

"Don't worry, Father," said the farmer's clever daughter. She hid in one of the baskets and covered the top with fruits. It looked as if it was full of fruits! The king's men took the basket, not noticing anything. At the castle, when nobody was looking, the daughter crept out of the basket and ran back home. Her father was spared!

29. Tanya and the Wolf

Tanya was a kind-hearted girl. One day, she ran into a wolf cub that was very weak. She fed him and took care of him. When he was healthy, she left him in the forest. As the years went by, Tanya forgot all about the little wolf cub.

One day, when she was walking through the forest, some goons sprang at her from behind the trees. There was nowhere to run.

Just then, a fierce-looking wolf sprang out from the trees and snarled at the goons. They ran away as fast as they could. Tanya was shocked. It was the same cub she had rescued all those years ago! The wolf nuzzled her lovingly. Tanya never had to walk through the forest alone again.

30. The Lost Needle

Sally was learning how to sew. Her mother told her to be especially careful with her needles, as they were sharp and could hurt people. Sally didn't pay much attention to what her mother had said. When she lost her needle, Sally didn't bother to look for it. Instead, she just bought a new one.

One day, Sally's mother sent her on some errands. All afternoon, Sally had to run around the market in the heat. When she returned home, Sally was very tired. She plopped on the porch chair. Immediately, she jumped up with a yelp. Her lost needle was stuck in her chair! From that day onwards, Sally was very careful with her needles.

31. Neil's Guitar

Neil had a magic guitar that would play by itself. Everyone loved his guitar and some were even jealous of Neil. One day, someone stole Neil's guitar.
The guitar was sleeping in its case when it was stolen. It only realised what had happened when the thief opened the case and took it out. The guitar wanted to go back to Neil's home. It didn't know what to do. So, it began playing itself on the top of its voice. The music was so shrill and loud that the whole town was able to hear it. The police quickly found the thief's house, rescued the guitar and returned it to Neil.

1. Bingo and the Butterfly

Bingo the puppy loved to play in the garden. His best friend was a caterpillar named Dizzy. They would play together every day. One day, when Bingo went out, he couldn't find Dizzy anywhere. Bingo spent all day searching for Dizzy, but he did not find her. He kept looking for many days. But Dizzy was nowhere to be seen! Bingo whimpered sadly. He missed his best friend. "Did she move to another garden?" he wondered. "I didn't even get to say goodbye!"

One day, when Bingo was sitting sadly with his head on his paws, a beautiful blue butterfly sat on his nose. Bingo was confused. He had never seen this butterfly before.

"Hi Bingo," it said. "Do you recognise me?" It was Dizzy! She had transformed into a lovely butterfly. Bingo was happy that his friend was back. They played happily and remained best friends for life.

189

2. The Glass of Water

Jeff bustled into his house, sweaty and tired after a game of football. While he was washing up, his mother poured him a glass of water and kept it on the table.

Jeff came to the table and drank the water. No sooner did he taste the water, than he spat it out and made a disgusted face.

His mother was shocked with his behaviour. "Why did you do that, Jeff?" she asked him crossly.

Jeff didn't say anything. He just motioned for his mother to taste the water. Jeff's mother took a small sip and she spat it out too! She had filled it with vinegar instead of water. Poor Jeff had almost swallowed an entire glass of vinegar!

190

3. Tracy's Toaster

Tracy's toaster was very strange. It was meant to toast bread, but when Tracy was not around, it would try to toast other things. Tracy would find it filled with popcorn, eggs and other foods that it had tried to toast. Tracy tried to warn the toaster that it would get hurt, but it would not listen.

One day, it tried to toast a packet of chewing gum!

The gum melted and got stuck to the toaster. No matter how much the toaster tried, it could not pop the gum out. It was jammed. When Tracy returned, she had to dismantle the toaster and clean it out. It took her all day. From that day onwards, Tracy's toaster stuck to toasting bread!

4. Miranda's Painting

Miranda's school was holding a painting competition. She had prepared a beautiful painting to enter into the competition. Miranda kept her painting on the table to dry under the ceiling fan. When she went to check on it, she was shocked. Her puppy had walked all over it and spread the paint around!

Miranda was distraught. The painting was completely ruined and she did not have time to redo it. Miranda had no choice but to take the messed-up painting to school the next day. When it was put up on the wall for display, she was sure she would not win any prize. You can imagine her surprise when she was announced as the winner!

Her painting looked very different and the judges thought it was modern art. Miranda thanked her puppy when she reached home.

5. What Holly Did

One evening, Holly came home and found an escaped convict sleeping on the armchair. The lights were off, so Holly could not see his face. But she could make out the pattern of his prison clothes. Nobody was home. Holly's parents were attending a function after watching her brother's school play. So Holly bound the convict's hands, feet and mouth with duct tape. When he woke up, he started struggling. At that moment, Holly's parents came home. They saw the convict and rushed to untie him. That was when Holly saw his face. It was her brother! He had come home, tired from his play and had fallen asleep without removing his prisoner costume!

6. The Dumpster Diver

Sarah was a very tidy girl. Everything in her room was always in its proper place.

Even Sarah's favourite doll, Amelia, would always be lying on her pillow. One day, Sarah came home from school to see that Amelia was gone. Sarah started to panic. She ran to her mother and asked if she had seen Amelia. "Hmm," said Sarah's mother, thinking hard. "I vacuumed your room clean today. It is possible that Amelia fell down and I vacuumed her by mistake."

Sarah began to think. The vacuum bags were now probably at the dumpster at the street corner. She put on her rubber gloves and went to the dumpster. Sarah poked around and finally found her doll. She took Amelia home and they both took a bath with disinfectant.

7. Agnes and the Seed

Agnes was vacationing in the mountains with her family.

One day, she came upon a cave that was frozen solid. Agnes stepped inside and saw some strange-looking frozen seeds lying in a corner. She put them in her pocket and took them home.

When Agnes got home, she planted the seeds in her garden and watered them every day. In a few days, small flower buds began to sprout. After a month, they bloomed into large blue flowers. They grew even taller than Agnes! Everyone wanted to know what kind of flowers they were, but Agnes had no idea. For all she knew, the seeds might have gotten frozen during the era of dinosaurs!

8. The Clever Farmer

One day, a poor farmer woke up to find his horse missing. He looked everywhere for his horse, but he did not find it. He decided to go to the market to buy a new one. But there, he saw a man selling his horse.

"Excuse me sir, this is my horse," said the farmer.

"Of course not!" replied the seller. "I've had him for two years now."

The farmer just smiled. He covered the horse's eyes with his hand. "If he's your horse," he said, "I'm sure you will be able to tell me which eye he is blind in!"

"Err...the left eye?" replied the man. It was just a guess. The farmer laughed. "Wrong!" he said. "My horse is not blind. See!" The farmer removed his hands from the horse's eyes. Sure enough, the horse had two healthy eyes. The clever farmer took him home.

193

9. The Angry Lake

There was once a lake that had a very bad temper. Instead of behaving nicely like all the other lakes, it would bubble and start boiling without any reason. None of the fish or ducks lived in it because it was so angry.

The people of the village were tired of it as well. They needed a new lake.

So they came up with a plan.

One day, when the lake was boiling away, they poured truckloads of jelly mix and fruit into it.

The boiling lake cooked the jelly mix. When it cooled down, it had become a huge blob of delicious jelly! Everyone brought huge jars and took some home to eat. When it rained, the lake filled up with new water. Everyone was happy again.

194

10. The Big Nose

Mr. Magoo had a dreadfully big nose. Everyone would make fun of him all the time. He hardly ever stepped out of his house. He had no friends.

One day, a thief stole all the mince pieces from the town bakery. The people had no way of finding out who did it. They thought hard to find a way to catch the thief.

"Why don't we ask Mr. Magoo?" said one person. "I'm sure he will be able to sniff out the pies."

Everybody went to Mr. Magoo and pleaded for his help. Mr. Magoo sniffed the pies out with his big nose and found the pie thief in no time. Since that day, everyone stopped making fun of his nose. They treated Mr. Magoo with respect.

11. Clumsy Calvin

Calvin was a nice young man, but he was very clumsy. When it was time to find a job, he was sure no one would hire him because of his clumsiness. But he decided to try his luck anyway. He put an advertisement in the newspaper which read: "A very clumsy man who breaks everything is looking for a job." To his surprise, he actually got a reply! Calvin's new job was at a toy factory that claimed to make unbreakable toys. Every new design was given to Calvin first. If he managed to break it, it was sent back for redesigning. Only if the toys passed Calvin's test would they be sold in the market. That's how clumsy Calvin found the perfect job!

195

12. Of Bunnies and Burrows

The Easter bunny was going around hiding chocolate eggs in gardens for children to find the next day. While he was hiding the eggs, he ate a lot of them as well. By dawn, he was tired and had become very fat. When he tried to go back to Bunny Land, the Easter bunny couldn't fit into his burrow.

He tried to climb in and got stuck!
He called out to Timmy, the boy who lived nearby. Timmy came running and laughed heartily at the Easter bunny. He then dug the soil around the burrow so that the bunny could fit inside and go home. In return for his help, the Easter bunny gave Timmy lots of extra chocolate eggs.

13. Jonelle's book

Jonelle was a budding writer. She wanted to write a book so that many children around the world would read it. The only problem was that Jonelle had no idea what to write about.

She decided to look for inspiration. So Jonelle walked in the park, went to the zoo and even waited in the dentist's office. But nothing seemed to give her any ideas!

After going back to her room and thinking about her day, she finally got an excellent idea. Jonelle wrote a story about a writer looking for ideas to write a book! The story she wrote was very interesting. Everyone liked it very much.

14. Fatcat

There was once a mean factory owner called Fatcat. He would make products of poor quality and sell them at high prices. What's more, he would not even pay his employees properly.

One day, Fatcat's employees decided to teach him a lesson. They went to his house and replaced all his expensive things with the cheap things that he made in the factory. When Fatcat got home that day and used his things, they either broke or didn't work properly.

When he looked at his things closely, he saw that they had all been replaced by things from his factory. Fatcat felt ashamed. From the next day onwards, he made sure that only good-quality products were manufactured in his factory. He also treated his employees better. Everyone was happy with the new Fatcat!

15. The Echo Chamber

Ronan was a big braggart. He loved to talk about himself all the time. Nobody ever got to talk about themselves when he was around. He would go on and on for hours.

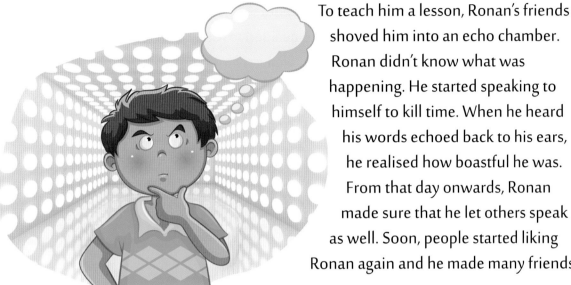

To teach him a lesson, Ronan's friends shoved him into an echo chamber. Ronan didn't know what was happening. He started speaking to himself to kill time. When he heard his words echoed back to his ears, he realised how boastful he was. From that day onwards, Ronan made sure that he let others speak as well. Soon, people started liking Ronan again and he made many friends.

16. Polly Saves the Day

The Wilson family had a pet parrot named Polly. They were teaching her to speak. So far, she had only learnt how to say "I see you" whenever she saw anyone. One Sunday, when the Wilsons had gone out, a thief climbed in through the window and looked around. He did not notice Polly sitting on the top of the cupboard. The thief began opening the drawers and cupboards. "I see you!" squawked Polly as he came nearer.

The thief jumped out of his skin. He looked around, but saw nobody. Polly kept repeating "I see you!" The thief thought it was a ghost watching him. He ran off as fast as his legs would allow him to! Polly the parrot had saved the day.

17. Counting Stars

Dr. Whizzbang was very worried. The Inventor's Convention was coming up and he had to invent a machine to count all the stars in the sky! If he did not succeed, he would be a laughing stock. Dr. Whizzbang was a genius, but his wife, Mrs. Whizzbang, was also extremely clever. "Don't worry," she said. "I have an idea." On the day of the convention, Dr. Whizzbang pressed the button to calculate the number of stars. A piece of paper slipped out from the chute. It read: "The number of stars is the same as the number of grains of sand on the beach." All the inventors laughed and applauded Dr. Whizzbang for the clever solution.

18. Denise and Sean

Denise and Sean loved to gossip and spread rumours about everyone they knew. Their friends got tired of their lies and decided to teach them a lesson. They went to Sean and told him that Denise called him a fat bully. Then, they went to Denise and told her that Sean called her a lazy cow. Both the friends got very angry with each other. They had a huge fight. By the time they realised that they were only rumours, both of them had already hurt each other. They decided to stop spreading lies about their friends.

19. Trapping the Scorpion

A new scorpion had come to the forest and was troubling all the other animals. He would chase them around the forest for fun, threatening them with his stinger.

One day, he was chasing a rabbit all around the forest. The rabbit was getting tired. It was almost at the edge of the forest, where the villagers in the nearby village were constructing a wall. The rabbit fell into a patch of wet cement. It was able to jump out quickly. But the scorpion could not crawl through the thick cement. It hardened while the scorpion was still struggling inside.

The rabbit went back to the forest and told all the animals how the scorpion was stuck at the construction site.

Everyone was happy to be rid of the mean scorpion.

20. How Ching Became Rich

Once upon a time, in ancient China, there lived a poor but clever boy named Ching. One day, the Emperor of China announced a task. Whoever could present him with a drum that beat by itself would be given a handsome reward.

Many people tried their luck. Magicians tried to enchant their drums. Rich people spent lots of money looking for ancient drums with magical powers. But none of them could beat by themselves.

Ching did not know magic. He did not have the money to travel and search for drums. But he was very clever. He came up with a plan. Ching released a swarm of bees into a tin can and trapped them inside. He covered the top and bottom of the drum with leather.

Whenever the 'drum' was picked up, the bees began to fly around, banging against the leather and making a beating sound.

The Emperor of China was so impressed that he gave Ching a big reward and made him his chief advisor. Ching was never poor again!

200

21. The Wild Ride

Ezra's mother had sent him to the supermarket with a long list of items to buy. One of the items was a broomstick. Ezra looked in all the aisles, but couldn't find a broomstick anywhere. Then, he spotted one kept near the coffee aisle. As soon as he touched it, it hovered off the ground and zoomed up to the ceiling, with Ezra hanging on! Everyone at the supermarket stared as the broomstick flew around. Ezra was scared, but he was also having fun! The broomstick actually belonged to a witch who had forgotten about it while shopping. She returned and commanded it to come down. Ezra had a great adventure because of her forgetfulness!

22. Down the Hole

Jose was playing with his football in the garden. He kicked it a little too hard and it went hurtling into the bushes. Jose ran after it, but it kept going farther away. It went straight down a rabbit hole! Jose sat down and reached into it. His fingers brushed against the football and pushed it deeper into the hole. Jose decided to go after it. When he climbed down, he saw rabbits scurrying about in a tiny city. When they saw Jose, they invited him to a party with them. Jose had lots of fun with the rabbits. He was glad his football had rolled into the hole.

23. The Royal Taster

The royal taster had a dangerous job. He had to taste everything that was to be served to the king. This was to make sure that nobody tried to poison the king's food. One day, the kingdom imported peanuts for the very first time. They had heard a lot about peanut butter and were eager to make their own. The king ordered his cooks to make him peanut butter. When it was made, the royal taster got the very first taste. It was so good, that he kept eating until he licked the jar clean!

When the king saw this, he was very angry. But the taster was a smart man. "Your majesty," he said. "I only ate the whole jar to save you from harm. What if you are allergic to peanuts?" The king decided to eat some peanuts and find out if he was allergic. Sure enough, he was! He broke out into an itchy rash.

It was the taster's sheer luck that the king turned out to be allergic to peanuts. Instead of being punished for his greediness, he was rewarded for his caution.

24. It's Raining!

Once upon a time, there were two elf brothers named Vilor and Vosha. They owned a shop where they sold umbrellas, raincoats, sweaters and sunglasses.

It so happened that the weather had been very pleasant. Nobody needed any umbrellas, raincoats or sunglasses. Vilor and Vosha were sad. Their business was not doing very well. They needed to make money. One day, the two elf brothers hatched a plan. Vilor sat on top of the tree with a watering can. Every time someone passed, he would tip the watering can so that they thought it was raining! They were forced to buy an umbrella from the shop from Vosha. After two days, Vilor and Vosha were very happy. They had made enough money to last them a while.

25. The Misunderstood Giant

Gigantus was a gentle-hearted giant. Nobody was afraid of him because he was very clumsy and awkward. Everyone, including little children, made fun of him. So Gigantus decided to teach everyone a lesson. He walked into the city and kidnapped little Julius, who had only one leg. Gigantus was going to kill him. This would make everyone afraid of him. "Don't do this," said Julius. "They make fun of me, too! I am different, too." Gigantus felt sad. He realised that everyone has problems. He sent Julius home. From that day onwards, Gigantus took pride in being the funny giant that everyone loved.

26. Magnetic Attraction

The people of Fermur used iron pieces as currency. They were honest people and never faced too many problems. But one day, a thief came to Fermur with strong magnets. His plan was to go close to people's pockets and wave the magnet.

The iron pieces would stick to the magnet and the thief would steal them. That night, he took two big magnets and went about his plan. He collected a lot from the shop cash registers, since no one was around to stop him. But the greedy man had attracted so much iron, that they too became magnetic. They got attracted to a large metal statue in the town square! No matter how much the thief tried to escape, he could not. He was caught and put in jail. If only he had left the magnets and ran, he would have saved himself!

27. Esther the Eel

Esther was an electric eel. She could electrocute the water around her and give everyone a shock. Most of her friends were a little scared of her, even though she was nice. Esther wanted to prove to everyone that she had her electricity under control and wouldn't harm anyone.

One day, a few mean people came with a boat and tried to capture all the fish. Esther knew this was her chance. She circled their boat and conducted her electricity only in that part. The boat got charged and sent shocks to everyone on it.

The mean thugs turned the boat around and ran back home. Esther used her electricity to save everyone!

28. The Suitcase

Mrs. Greyson was going on a holiday with her husband. She had packed all their things into one big suitcase and now she had to close it. But the suitcase was over-stuffed and would not close! Mrs. Greyson tried everything. She shuffled her things, removed a few items and squeezed as much as she could. Finally, Mrs. Greyson sat on the lid. She made her husband sit on it, too. Together, they pressed down and tried to force the lid closed.

But alas, they ended up breaking the suitcase! Mr. and Mrs. Greyson were left sitting on their clothes through the massive crack they had made. The couple had a good laugh at their own expense.

205

29. Camelot the Chameleon

Camelot the chameleon was a master of disguises. He was also a very good detective. One day, he was requested to investigate the bear, who was always sneaking off every afternoon. Camelot decided to see where he went. He jumped from tree to tree, always merging with the colour of the bark. The bear walked right to the edge of the forest and went into a cave. Inside the cave, Camelot saw that he had stored many boxes of firecrackers. The bear planned to light them everywhere in the forest and scare everyone. That night, Camelot took the firecrackers and lit them in the bear's cave. The bear got a fright! He ran outside as fast as he could. He never played mean tricks again.

30. Trisha's Dog

Trisha had a big, brown dog that was very loyal to her. He was also very beautiful. The King of the Underworld saw Trisha's dog and stole him away. He wanted him to be the guardian of the Gates of the Underworld.

Trisha was very angry to see her dog stolen. She decided to teach the King of the Underworld a lesson. Taking a backpack with supplies, Trisha made her way to the Underworld. She sneaked into the king's castle and snooped around. The King of the Underworld had pet birds. Trisha unlocked the cages and released all the birds.

Just as she was finished, the King of the Underworld stepped in angrily. "What have you done?" he asked. "Those were my beloved pets!"

"Serves you right!" shouted Trisha. "Now you know what it feels like to lose a pet!" Trisha took her dog home and the cranky king spent the next few days looking for his pet birds.

1. Dario's New Home

Dario was an elf who lived in a mushroom by the river. One day, it rained very heavily and the river got flooded. The water spilled onto the bank and took Dario's house with it. The little elf didn't know what to do. He liked his mushroom house very much. Feeling sad, he went in search of a new place to live.

As he was walking, Dario saw a big pumpkin by the bushes. It was crying bitterly.

"What's the matter?" asked Dario, kindly.

"I was carved into a jack-o-lantern for Halloween," sobbed the pumpkin. "But now that Halloween is over, I've been thrown away!"

Dario smiled as an idea formed in his mind. "I'm looking for a new house," he said."How would you like it if I lived inside you? That way, we can both be happy."

The pumpkin thought it was a great idea. He was very happy to be a home to this kind elf. That's how Dario came to live inside a pumpkin!

207

2. Solomon and the Witch

Solomon was walking home from work one night. It was very late and he had missed the last bus. He had no choice but to wait for someone to give him a ride.

He stuck out his thumb, waiting for a car to stop.

Finally, he saw a red car slowing down. It was driven by a lady who looked harmless and kind. Solomon got into the car happily. As she drove away, he saw her reflection in the rear-view mirror. To his shock, he saw that she was actually a witch!

Solomon decided to run out of the car at his first chance. When the car stopped at a traffic signal, he opened the door and jumped out. But just as he was leaving, the witch made a grab at him. "Not so fast!" she said. "I need your hair for my potions!"

The witch tugged really hard at Solomon's hair. His wig came off in her hands!

Solomon ran away as fast as he could. He had always hated his baldness. But it saved his life that day!

208

3. The Bake Sale

A bake sale had been organised by the Little Girls' Book Club. The girls planned to sell cookies and lemonade to raise money to buy a new set of books.

Sasha was in charge of the cookies. She baked them with her mother's help and set them out to cool. When it was time to dust them with sugar, Sasha used the salt by mistake. She did not realise her mistake until people began to eat them. They were so salty! That day, the girls didn't sell many cookies. But they did sell lots of lemonade! Everyone who ate the cookies immediately wanted lemonade to get rid of the taste. They ended up making enough money to buy the books they wanted.

209

4. How the Conch Trapped the Sea

The sea spirit wanted to take a vacation. He asked the conch shell to take him to the mountains for a few days. The conch agreed and the sea spirit entered inside it. They rolled to the shore together. From there, a seagull lifted them up into the mountains. After a few days, the sea spirit was relaxed and ready to go back into the sea. But the conch refused to let him go. "You will stay trapped inside me forever!" it said. The sea spirit put on a brave struggle. Finally, he managed to escape. But a little part of him remains with the conch shell till today. If you put your ear to a conch, you will hear the sea spirit whispering inside.

5. Lock and Key

Jason had just moved into his new house. His mother tossed him a large bunch of keys. "Open all the doors," she said. "Let the house air out."

Jason took the bunch of keys and opened the doors, one by one. It was a difficult task, because he had to try many different keys before he got the right one. It took him all morning. Finally, only one door was left.

"This will be easy," thought Jason. "I only have one more key!" But when he inserted the last key into the keyhole, it refused to click open. Jason tried to insert it from every angle until he was thoroughly tired. He called his mother for help. Jason's mother simply turned the handle and pushed the door open! All along, Jason had been trying to unlock a door that was already unlocked!

6. The Monkey Trap

A poacher wanted to capture the monkeys of Bonbon Forest and make them work in a shoe factory. He decided to build a trap. He dug a pit and covered it with a layer of grass and a few bananas. Then, he waited for the monkeys to fall into the trap.

But the poacher didn't know that some monkeys had been watching everything from a tree. The clever monkeys came up with a plan of their own. That day, not a single monkey fell into the poacher's trap. He decided to come back on the next day. But when he came back to the forest the next day, the entire path had been covered with banana peels. The evil man slipped on the peels and fell straight into his own pit! The monkeys could not stop laughing at him.

7. The Dust Bunnies

Brittany was very messy. Her things were scattered all over her room. Her mother kept asking her to clean the room, but she wouldn't listen.

One day, Brittany found a bunch of cute little rabbits coming from under her bed! "We are the dust bunnies," they said. "And if you don't clean your room, we will take over it!" Brittany just laughed. What could these cute little bunnies do?

The dust bunnies kept growing in number, until they had completely covered Brittany's room. She could barely walk without stepping on their little tails. Brittany thought of how she could make the dust bunnies go away. "Ah-ha!" she said. "I'll use the vacuum cleaner."

Brittany brought the vacuum cleaner and cleaned away the bunnies. But there were so many! She had to clean every little corner and put all her things back in their proper place. When that was done, she caught all the dust bunnies in no time.

Brittany was thrilled! Not only did she defeat the dust bunnies, but she also found a pair of missing earrings, a bottle of perfume, a lost board game and her favourite pair of socks she thought she had lost forever.

8. The Fossil

There once lived a seashell who wanted to be famous. His dream was to be the centre of everyone's attention. He tried writing, singing, dancing and acting, but nothing made him famous. One day, he climbed to the top of a cliff. He decided to jump into the sea to create a world record of jumping from the highest point.

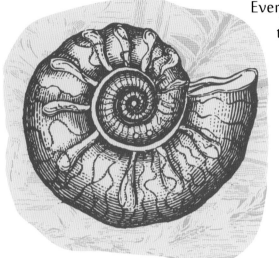

Everyone waited below on the seashore for him to make the jump. As the seashell jumped in, he dislodged a rock from its place. The seashell fell on into the sea and the rock settled on top of him, sandwiching him into a fossil. For years, he remained there, until someone found him and put him into a fossil museum. The seashell finally got to be the centre of attraction. He lived happily ever after as an artefact.

9. The Grumpy Chair

The grumpy old leather chair was everyone's favourite. There was always someone making themselves comfortable on him.
The chair was tired of getting smashed by everyone's sweaty behinds!
He decided to push his springs out so that no one would disturb him anymore. People stopped sitting on him. At first, the chair was very happy. But then he grew sad and lonely. When he was repaired at last, he made it a point to not be grumpy. Whenever anyone sat on him, he always made sure they were very comfortable.

10. The Red Ball

Mickey was a naughty boy who had a bad habit of snooping around. One day, he went to a witch's house and peered in through her window. Mickey saw that she had a magical red ball that did whatever she asked. When the witch left the room, Mickey sneaked inside her house and grabbed the ball.

To his surprise, the ball turned into a big, red balloon! It began floating and bobbed straight out of the window. At first, it was exciting. But then, the balloon went even higher! Mickey started yelling at the top of his lungs. The witch heard the commotion and came running outside. She brought Mickey back to the ground and let him run home. He had been punished enough!

213

11. Catching the Thief

One night, while Mr. Danbury was having a dinner party, his wife found that her pearl necklace was stolen. The Danburys hired Claude the detective to catch the thief.

Claude questioned everyone who was present at the party. But he still didn't know who the thief was. He thought of an idea. He asked all the suspects to stand in a line.

"I have a magic powder," said Claude. "When I sprinkle it, the thief's nose will become longer." Claude didn't have magic powder. He just sprinkled his snuff powder. But sure enough, one person touched their nose.

At once, Claude had that man arrested.

12. Down the Drain

Elise had a pet mouse named Pepper. One day, she was trying to bathe him, but Pepper was struggling to get away. Because he was slippery with soap, Pepper went flying into the toilet bowl! He slid down the pipes and into the sewer.

The sewer was large and scary. Pepper was sure he would never be able to find his way back. Just then, he saw an old ball floating down the sewer. He hopped on it and waited to see where it would go. As the ball floated, he saw a tiny exit along one wall.

Pepper jumped off the ball and climbed out. To his luck, the opening led into a gutter near Elise's house! Elise was happy to see him, but had to give him another bath.

13. The Cheater

Whenever Benji played cards with his friends, he would always try to cheat. Sometimes, he would switch his cards with the ones in the deck. At other times, he would peek into his friends' cards. All his friends were tired of Benji's antics. They wanted to teach him a lesson.

So one day, as they sat together to play, Benji's friends arranged the cards in such a way that Benji got the worst hand. No matter what he did, Benji just could not win! He was not used to losing and felt very sad. Then his friends explained what they had done. Benji realised his mistake and promised to never cheat again.

14. The Mighty Tree

A mango seed was sitting on the kitchen table, lost in thought. It was dreaming of becoming a mighty tree. But it could not do that unless it took root. How was it going to take root on a kitchen table? The seed waited patiently for an opportunity.

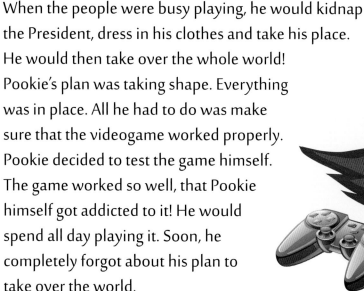

The next day, when the kids were leaving for school, the mango seed jumped into one of their backpacks.

On the way to the bus stop, a car whizzed by. The seed fell out and landed on its hood.

The car stopped near a football field. This was the seed's chance! It jumped off and took root in the field. Many years later, it grew into a mighty mango tree. It lived a happy life!

215

15. Pookie's Plan

Pookie the parrot was an evil mastermind. He wanted to take over the planet and make humans his slaves. He would plot and scheme against people all day. His latest plan involved getting all the humans hooked to an addictive videogame about birds.

When the people were busy playing, he would kidnap the President, dress in his clothes and take his place. He would then take over the whole world! Pookie's plan was taking shape. Everything was in place. All he had to do was make sure that the videogame worked properly. Pookie decided to test the game himself. The game worked so well, that Pookie himself got addicted to it! He would spend all day playing it. Soon, he completely forgot about his plan to take over the world.

16. The Kite's Flight

The toys in Nelson's toy cupboard were always mean to the kite. The action figures made fun of it for not having a gun. The remote-control cars made fun of it for being a lightweight. The toy blocks laughed at its funny shape and flat body. Teddy laughed at it because it had no hands and legs.

The kite was sad and spent most of its time alone in a corner. One windy day, Nelson finally took it out of the cupboard and to the park. Nelson's kite soared high in the air. It could touch the clouds!

The kite looked at the ground. Everything looked so small. All the other toys were standing at the window, staring at it enviously. The kite smiled to itself. It was happy.

17. The Flying Umbrella

Arion the wizard was working on a magical flying potion. It was Arion's dream to be able to fly. Finally, Arion's potion was complete! He went all around the laboratory, dancing with joy. But Arion was a very clumsy wizard. He accidentally bumped into the cauldron and sent his potion crashing to the ground. It spilt all over his umbrella stand. Before Arion could scoop up the potion, his umbrella absorbed it all. The wizard was upset. Not only did he waste his potion, he also ruined his umbrella! But when he opened it to dry, it carried him up in the air! The wizard's dream had come true. His potion worked after all!

18. The Tiny Rat

Binky was the tiniest rat in his big family. Everyone made fun of his small size and called him names. This made Binky sad.

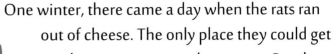

One winter, there came a day when the rats ran out of cheese. The only place they could get cheese now was at the rat trap. But they all knew that whoever would go to the rat trap would get caught in it.

Binky looked at the rat trap. He noticed that it was built for big rats. Someone as small as him could easily take the cheese and get away. Binky jumped on the rat trap and successfully managed to take the piece of cheese home. No one said a word about his size from that day onwards.

217

19. Knutty and the Hunter

The forest animals all lived in harmony, but they had one enemy—Monty the hunter. One day, Monty captured Knutty the bear. He nailed him into a crate and put him

on a train to the city. The animals held a council meeting to try and save Knutty. They came up with a plan and decided to go ahead with it. All the elephants of the jungle stood at the train tracks. Seeing the elephants, the train came to a halt. Then, the monkeys started to look for Knutty. When they found him, the beavers broke open the cage with their teeth. That's how the animals helped Knutty escape! They all celebrated their success with a party.

20. The Lion Who Loved to Sing

Ben loved animals. And nobody knew that he could actually speak to them! That's why Ben was very excited when his mother took him to the zoo. He was looking forward to making new animal friends.

They saw many different animals. Some of them were friendly and they told Ben many interesting stories. Some of them were too busy to chat with Ben. And some others were snoring away when Ben went to meet them!

But when Ben reached the lion's cage, he was awestruck. "What a majestic beast!" he thought. "I must go and speak to him." Ben slipped between the legs of the people standing in front and made his way to the very front of the cage.

The lion walked right up to Ben. "Why aren't you scared of me, little boy?" he asked. "Because you aren't scary," replied Ben.

"I know," sighed the lion. "I can't understand why people are so scared of me! All I want to do is sing!"

The lion took a deep breath, opened his mouth and broke into a song. Ben's mother screamed. She thought the lion was growling! She grabbed Ben and pulled him away from the front of the cage. Ben didn't bother trying to explain that the poor lion was only trying to sing. She wouldn't believe him anyway!

21. Candyfloss Land

One morning, Finn woke up with a smile on his face. He had just had a wonderful dream about a magical place. It was called Candyfloss Land, and it was filled with clouds of candyfloss! Finn made up his mind to find this place.

"Excuse me," he asked the passersby. "Do you know how I can get to Candyfloss Land?" But they all just looked at him strangely! Nobody could help him out. Finn went back home, feeling very dejected. His mother was sad to see him dejected. She decided to cheer him up by giving him his favourite snack—candyfloss! As he was eating, Finn was struck by an idea. It was a little silly, but he decided to give it a try.

Finn looked at the half-eaten candyfloss in his hand. "Er…" he said. "Do you know how I can get to Candyfloss Land?"

For a moment, nothing happened. Then, to his utmost surprise, the candyfloss began to delicately unravel itself from the stick.

It formed a long, cloudy path!

Finn began walking up the path. It went up the mountains and through the clouds, until it finally reached Candyfloss Land. Finn was overjoyed. He spent lots of time there, having fun and eating candyfloss. Then he took the path back and went home.

219

22. The Dental Disaster

Peter sat in the dentist's waiting room, nervously awaiting his turn. He did not like dentists at all. When it was his turn to go in, he stole a glance at the boy coming out. He had a strange, blank look on his face. He simply looked straight ahead and walked out without a word.

When he entered the dentist's room, Peter found that he, too, had the same blank look and robotic movements! He started to get suspicious. As he climbed into the chair, he gasped! Perched on the cupboard was a slimy green alien!

While the dentist was washing his hands, Peter took one of his sharp tools and held it in his hand. As soon as the dentist told him to open his mouth wide, the alien jumped down. But Peter was ready. He stuck the dentist's tool into the alien's stomach. The creature screeched and disappeared into thin air.

Just then, the life returned into the dentist's eyes. He had no idea what had happened and Peter didn't bother telling him. After all, he wasn't going to believe him anyway!

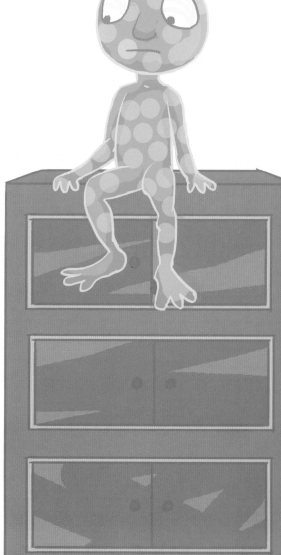

23. The Mystery of the Missing Necklace

Hazel couldn't find her necklace anywhere. It was her favourite necklace, too! She decided to calm down and put on her thinking cap. It was time for detective work!

She began retracing her steps since she last saw her necklace. Last night, she had attended her friend's party. When she got home, she was very tired and did not bother to take off her necklace. She kept it on and went to bed. In the morning, the necklace was gone. Hazel stood at the window, thinking hard. Then she saw her necklace! It was in a cuckoo's nest. The cuckoo had gotten attracted to the sparkling necklace and had stolen it by entering her window.

24. Mother Mouse

Once upon a time, there lived a mother mouse with her baby. They lived in a hole in the wall of a big, warm house with lots of cheese. One day, Mother Mouse decided to take her baby outside. Waiting for them was a huge ginger tomcat, licking its lips and waiting to eat them both up. "What should we do?" cried the baby. Mother Mouse just smiled. She was not afraid at all. She knew exactly how to deal with big, scary cats.

She opened her mouth and took in a deep breath. "Woof! Woof! Bark bark bark!" she shouted. The cat heard the sound and ran away as fast as he could!

25. Planet Morbo

Tamsin was walking on the street when aliens from Planet Morbo captured her and put her in prison. They wanted to ransom her for all the chocolate on Earth.

Tamsin knew she had to escape. She called out to her guard and asked him to free her.

"Do I look stupid to you?" asked the mean guard.

"Of course not," replied Tamsin. "You look very smart. But can you get me something fizzy to drink? And a few mints to chew on."

Believing her flattery, the guard brought her what she wanted. Tamsin popped the mints into the bottle of fizzy soda and began to shake it.

Finally, the bottle burst open with a loud 'POP!'

The door burst open with the explosion. Tamsin ran out before anyone could catch her and flew back to Earth.

26. Nigel's Shadow

Nigel would always try to sneak out at night, looking for something interesting to do. He wanted to have a night time adventure! One night, as he was going down, he was stopped by a dark figure.

"Who are you?" Nigel asked.

"I am your shadow," answered the figure. "In the day, I am stuck to you, but at night I am free. Let's go on an adventure!"

Nigel climbed onto his shadow's back and they flew out of the window, into the starry night sky. Nigel touched the clouds and the stars. He waved to the men on the Moon. He had a whale of a time! Finally, at the crack of dawn, his shadow brought him back to his room through his window.

27. Chloe and the Pearl

Chloe was walking along the seashore, looking for something. A crab was watching her curiously. He scuttled up to her. "What are you looking for, ma'am?" he asked. "I'm looking for oysters," replied little Chloe. "I want to find a pearl to give my mother." "Follow me," said the crab. He grabbed Chloe's sock with his claw and led her under the sea. Soon, they came to a huge factory which had a board on top saying 'Pearl Factory'. They went in and saw hundreds of oysters hard at work. There were different assembly lines, each producing a pearl of a different colour.

"Chloe wants a pearl to give her mother," said the crab to the oysters. The generous oysters allowed Chloe to choose any pearl that she liked.

"I like the pink one!" said Chloe. The pearl was very beautiful. Chloe thanked the oysters and also the crab for his help. Chloe's mother loved the gift, but she did not believe the fantastic story of how she managed to acquire it!

223

28. The Dream Seller

Every day, the dream seller would walk down Daisy's street, wearing his red coat and ringing his bell. "Give me your nightmares!" he would cry. "And I will give you sweet dreams in return!"

Daisy had a horrible nightmare, and was waiting for the dream seller eagerly. Finally, she saw him in the distance. She ran out to meet him. "Do you have any nightmares for me?" he asked her kindly.

Daisy nodded and whispered her nightmare into his ear.

The dream seller heard her patiently. "Thank you for your nightmare," he said. "In return, I promise that you will have a nice dream tonight." When Daisy fell asleep at night, she dreamt she was a princess who only ate ice cream.

29. The Quicksand

Ian had been warned not to go wandering all by himself, but he never listened. One day, while on a camping trip, he fell straight into a quicksand bog. Ian was in a fix. He began struggling to pull himself out of the quicksand. But the more he struggled, the deeper he was sucked in.

Finally, Ian got tired. He stopped wriggling and called out for help. His parents had realised he was missing and were searching for him when they heard him call out. They tied a rope to the car and made Ian hold the free end. With the strength of the car, they managed to drag him out.

Ian came out wet and scared. He was going to be more careful from now on.

30. The Echo Point

In the forest was a cliff that served as an echo point. Anything said there would get repeated. All the animals passing by would amuse themselves by saying things just to hear their voices echo back.

One day, the fox went to the cliff and said "Aeeooo!" But to his surprise, the echo point replied, "You're silly! Booooo!" The echo was insulting him! The fox figured out that something was wrong on the opposite cliff. He went there to check it out. He saw a group of naughty goblins with a microphone, laughing at him. The fox chased away the goblins and the echo point went back to normal!

31. Lucky Dylan

Dylan was a boy who lived by the edge of the forest. He would often wander into the jungle even though his mother told him not to.

One day, Dylan's mother gave him a new toy. It was one of those trick boxes which, when opened, actually punches the person opening it. Dylan ran through the forest to show his new toy to his friend Miles, who lived on the other side.

As he was walking, he saw a lion charging at him. Dylan didn't know what to do! He dropped the box and started running away. Suddenly, the lion's footsteps stopped. Dylan heard a loud roar. The lion had stepped on the box, got punched and was knocked out!

ISBN: 978-93-84225-31-5

ISBN: 978-81-87107-53-8

ISBN: 978-81-87107-55-2

ISBN: 978-81-87107-52-1

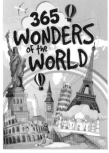

ISBN: 978-93-80069-35-7

ISBN: 978-93-80070-84-1

ISBN: 978-93-80070-83-4

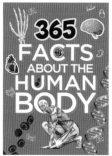

ISBN: 978-93-84625-93-1

ISBN: 978-93-83202-81-2

ISBN: 978-93-52760-49-7

ISBN: 978-81-87107-57-6

ISBN: 978-93-85031-29-8

ISBN: 978-93-84225-33-9

ISBN: 978-93-80070-79-7

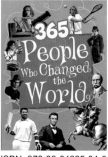

ISBN: 978-93-84225-34-6

ISBN: 978-81-87107-56-9

ISBN: 978-93-84625-92-4

ISBN: 978-81-87107-58-3

ISBN: 978-93-80069-36-4

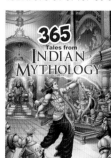

ISBN: 978-81-87107-46-0